20170759V

CW00644508

Six-gun Prodigal

Lew Clennan returned to Tinkettle Basin with a price on his head, a six-gun on his hip and a grudge. His bushwhacked father and brothers lay in their graves in the basin, where the vicious code of the grass-war now held sway.

Clennan rode a jump ahead of the bounty hunters to buck landgrabber Eli Brix, his gunhawks and crooked hangers-on. Pretty soon the whole basin knew that the six-gun prodigal was back on the scene in pursuit of vengeance.

Six-gun Prodigal

Ken Brompton

A Black Horse Western

ROBERT HALE · LONDON

ISBN-10: 0-7090-8144-8
ISBN-13: 978-0-7090-8144-9

Robert Hale Limited
Clerkenwell House
Clerkenwell Green
London EC1R 0HT

Typeset by
Derek Doyle & Associates, Shaw Heath
Printed and bound in Great Britain by
Antony Rowe Limited, Wiltshire

CHAPTER ONE

HOMECOMING

Under the brim of his hat the man had dark, bushy brows, pulled down in a menacing glower. His eyes were mere slits and his mouth a cruel slash. He was a spectacle to frighten children and ladies of a nervous disposition.

Beneath the crude woodcut depicting this disturbing vision, ran a legend in capitals:

SOUGHT BY THE
TRILLING DETECTIVE AGENCY
FOR MURDER, ATTEMPTED MURDER
AND ESCAPE FROM LEGAL CUSTODY:
LEW CLENNAN.
$500 REWARD POSTED BY MUNICIPAL
AUTHORITIES OF PURPLE FLATS,
TEXAS.
WARNING: CLENNAN IS LIKELY TO RESIST
ARREST BY USE OF FIREARMS

5

Lew Clennan, mounted on a dun-coloured bronc, considered the poster, nailed to a tree beside the trail, pulled a wry face, shook his head disbelievingly and said to the horse: 'If I thought I really looked like that sorry attempt at portraiture, I'd spend my life with a flour-sack over my head. At least I don't have to worry about anyone recognizing me from it. The stuff about murder and attempted murder is hogwash but they did get two things right – I did bust loose from the lawmen in Purple Flats and I will shoot if anyone tries to arrest me.'

With a sardonic smile, he reached forward and ripped the coarse paper reward dodger from the tree, screwed it up and cast it to the ground.

Only in the lean aspect of his face did the attempt to portray him come close to any resemblance to the real Lew Clennan. He had sunburned skin, tightened over the bones of a face whose sharpness had been brought on by hard experience and rough living but, at nearing thirty and with grey touching his temples, he was still a handsome man. By no means would his true appearance frighten children or ladies of a nervous disposition. He wore range gear, much punished by travel, and a Colt .45 was holstered low at his hip. Lew Clennan had a headlong and reckless past and he was fast with a gun. Though not by choice a gunslinger, recent events had set afoot a widespread rumour that he was one.

For all its inaccuracies, the reward dodger was disturbing. For this was not Texas, it was Arizona and Clennan was heading homeward to Tinkettle Basin. The fact that the poster had appeared here in Arizona Territory meant that the Trillings had second-guessed him. They must have somehow figured that he'd make for this region where Arizona merged with the Mexican border. Maybe they had even sent a man – or more than one man – ahead of him. And, right now, the last thing Clennan wanted was to tangle with the Trilling Detective Agency.

He touched spurs to his mount to urge it into a walk. Maybe the place was plastered with such posters, he thought – what a hell of a homecoming! Even so, he would not go into hiding or take on a false name. Too many people hereabouts knew him and the Clennan name carried some honour in this country. Everyone would soon know that Lew Clennan was back on the desert-edge ranges, now sweltering under a brassy May sun, because he aimed to make big trouble for a certain crew hereabouts.

The heat was strengthening towards its noontime height as Clennan angled his mount off the trail and crested a rise of scrubland. He halted and looked down into the pleasant spread of Tinkettle Basin. There it lay, surprisingly green for desert rim country due to the benefits bestowed by the waters of Tinkettle Creek, snaking lazily under the heat haze. West of the basin lay the lands of the MC ranch that his father had carved out, sweated to maintain and, finally, died in defending. In that land, too, were the graves of his brothers, Frank and Ed: bushwhack graves, for they also had met violent deaths in preserving the holdings inherited from their father.

At this time of day and under this sun, the basin appeared smiling and inviting, looking what it was: good country, the best cow country this portion of Arizona Territory could offer.

There was no indication of the dark and bloody menace which lay over the land – the menace of the voracious land-grabber, Eli Brix, who had gone a fair way towards achieving his ambition of building a cattle empire here and who was all too ready to use force, employing a collection of border gunhawks. It was three years since Lew Clennan had last seen the basin, three years in which Brix had furthered his avaricious ends, extending the holdings of his Slanted B ranch by running a couple of smaller outfits off the range. One was the MC, acquired after Frank and Ed, who had run the outfit since the violent death of their father, were lured into a gun-trap and shot down.

Looking east, Clennan saw the smudge of blue smoke over the huddled buildings of the town of Brimstone; then, swinging his gaze yet further east, he saw the splodge of green land on the edge of scrub where Lars Lundgren ran his small horse ranch.

'Things might have changed considerably but I always figured Lars was darned near immortal,' he muttered and turned his horse's nose in the direction of the horse ranch.

Three-quarters of an hour later he was riding up

the dusty roadway towards the weatherbeaten old cabin that Lars called home. The door of the cabin swung open and Lars stepped out on to the porch. Clennan could see he was older but he'd lost none of his bulk. Nor had he lost his strong accent for all he had left his birthplace, Sweden, many years before.

'Lew Clennan,' he roared. 'By God, I'd know you anywhere! I was watching through the window and saw you ride up. I was thinking how much you look like your father, the best, straightest and most honest man I ever knew.'

'And wondering why I didn't turn out as straight and honest, I'll warrant, Lars,' commented Clennan, dismounting.

'I don't take any account of that,' said Lars. 'If folk around here want to think one of Mark Clennan's sons has turned bad, let 'em think it. Circumstances dictate the course of a man's life. I know – I had my own wild times in Montana, long before I came here and I admit it. You'll always be welcome here. Water your horse at the trough around the corner and put him in the empty corral back of the house. There's good graze in there. Then step in. I have stew on the stove as it happens.'

In corralling his horse, Clennan looked over the stock of horses and ponies in the neat corrals at the rear of the cabin. Whatever else was going on in Tinkettle country, Lars Lundgren's enterprise looked pretty healthy, he reflected.

Inside the cabin, with its bachelor untidiness, he

found Lars cutting chunks from a large loaf of bread. The old Swede waved his guest to a seat at the scuffed board table then busied himself at a pot bubbling on the corner stove.

'You'll have Frank and Ed on your mind,' he said over his shoulder in tones less hearty than when he had welcomed Clennan.

'Sure, and I want to thank you for all you did. I heard you stepped in and arranged the funerals without giving a damn for Brix and his bunch. I'll pay you back for it.'

Lars Lungren shrugged. 'No need. It was the least I could do considering the respect I had for your father.' He paused, then added weightily, framing it as a question: 'You'll maybe have a mind to pay back other people in another kind of way, though?' He filled two bowls with hot stew, and shoved one across the table to Clennan, then gave him a helping of bread.

'Maybe,' said Clennan.

'It won't be easy. You'll have a lot stacked against you, bucking Brix's roughnecks. He's grown real powerful in this country since you left.'

'I already have plenty stacked against me, Lars. The Trillings are on my trail.'

'Hell!' exploded Lars. 'How far behind you are they?'

'I don't know. They might even be in front of me. I found a reward dodger nailed to a tree back yonder so they've put the word out this way, if they haven't sent a man or a squad of 'em.'

'One man against the Trillings *and* Eli Brix –

10

and don't tell me you don't plan to even up with Brix because that would be contrary to your history. It's a hell of a tall order, Lew', said Lars. 'I'd hate to see the last of the Clennan family wiped out. And, make no mistake about it, such law as there is here is controlled by Brix. He's built something of an empire here. If either Brix's gunsharps or the Trillings don't kill you, they'll hang you in Brimstone because Brix will contrive it that way.'

Clennan ate for a spell, then said flatly: 'Just the same, I aim to do something about Frank and Ed, and my old man too, and about the way Brix took over the MC. It's something I ought to have done a long time ago but for being otherwise engaged. I should have been here to stand with Frank and Ed all along. To my shame, I wasn't.'

'It's a hell of a call for one man alone,' Lars said. 'Brix has gathered a lot of power since you left, the sort of power that carries weight with politicians. He can hand out bribes in high places and he's not making his money from cattle alone. He's going strong on minerals now.'

'Minerals?'

'Yes. Silver. There was a fellow named Harry Siggs trying to run a little outfit beyond your place at the south end of the basin. He came in since your time. It wasn't much of a place, with very little stock, but Siggs had legal title to the land. Then, by some miracle, he struck silver on the place and was fool enough to let it be known around Brimstone. It seems Brix got word of it. Next thing, there was

11

a raiding party attacking Siggs's place one night, burning it out and running Siggs off. I heard he died somewhere. Maybe it's true a man can die of a broken heart. Brix now has a fair mining operation going there worked by poor Mexicans and Indians who're grateful for miserable wages.'

Lars rose and crossed to the stove where he started to prepare coffee. 'The opposition is very heavy, Lew,' he said. 'Brix is no longer just a tough pusher with a set of hired guns. He's getting to be a damned emperor with some mighty ugly gunsharps at his back. And he controls what passes for law in the Tinkettle country.'

'Even the most powerful emperor can be toppled,' replied Clennan.

'It's easy to say that but a damned sight harder to do it, even if you have the best-laid plan,' Lars said. 'Come to that, where do you plan to bunk down tonight if you've just arrived? Not that you can't stay here for as long as you have a mind to.'

'Thanks for the offer, Lars, but maybe just for tonight and no longer. I don't want either Brix's crew or the Trillings turning their attentions to you,' said Clennan.

The old Swede shrugged. 'They won't bother me. I'm on the fringe of Brix's territory and he has nothing to gain from shoving me. It's not as if I have any prime pastures worth stealing, just grass enough to keep this place running at a reasonable level. As a matter of fact, I'm in a good position to know what's going on in the basin. Folks come and go, buying horseflesh, and I hear most of the gossip. Not that I ever deal with the Slanted B. Brix seems to do all his horse-dealing over in Benson. As for the Trillings, they'll get nothing from me if they come nosing around.'

'I know that, Lars. Just the same, I'm keeping a tight mouth about what I aim to do. I don't want to bring any trouble to the decent folk in Tinkettle Basin. The less that's known about me the better.'

'I understand,' said Lars gravely. 'But take a word of warning. Keep out of Brimstone. Eli Brix owns the whole damned town now. He won't stop short of having you hanged there and he'll probably try to beat the Trillings to it. He won't like the last of the Clennans showing up – especially with the reputation you've acquired.'

Lew Clennan gave a quirky smile. 'I guess word of my reputation, as you call it, has been spread pretty thickly around the basin. I wonder how much of it is true and how much is overblown, making me into the ogre on a certain reward dodger.'

'Well, tales got around about a shooting scrape in Texas with a man killed and a break from jail and that seemed to automatically brand you as turning into a badman,' Lars told him. 'I don't know how much of it is true but I reckon most of it is overblown, which is the way of such stories. I know all the worthwhile folks in Tinkettle Basin who knew you were unwilling to believe you'd turned wanton killer. I never believed it, either. I don't want to know the how and why of it. I'm just glad to see you.'

13

'Thanks for having faith in me,' said Clennan. 'Without going into the details, I can tell you that what you heard is broadly true but I never went looking for trouble. I was a fool for putting too much time and energy into hoorawing around elsewhere when I should have been here, backing Frank and Ed. We should have stood together and formed a plan again Brix and his ambitions. Instead, I fought with my brothers, stormed out on them and headed for the high hills.'

'That's the impetuosity of youth,' Lars said tolerantly. 'Hardly a man alive doesn't go through that kind of phase. I was no exception myself. More coffee?'

Clennan shoved his cup across the table for a refill and Lars added: 'I figure I know why you're back here, Lew but, again, I'll remind you to go cautious. You'll have a lot stacked against you if you aim to buck Brix and the Slanted B with the Trillings on your tail to boot.'

When he rode off Lars Lundgren's place early the following morning, Lew Clennan still had not divulged any of his plans to the old horse-rancher. From the porch, Lars watched him go, thinking how much he resembled his father in appearance, though he plainly had not yet acquired Mark Clennan's reasonable approach to life, or his sober judgement.

But what had Mark Clennan's reasonable approach resulted in? reflected Lars. *Nothing but his murder and, ultimately, the bushwhacking of two of his three sons. And there was no doubt that it was all the work of Eli Brix, owner of the Slanted B outfit.*

As Clennan's dust dwindled in his backtrail, the old horse-rancher thought about the way things were in Tinkettle Basin before Brix arrived. The Slanted B was called the S Bar B in those days, the biggest spread in the basin region, owned by old Sam Ballinger, a tough and crusty old Arizona pioneer who'd fought Apaches in his time. He was a cattleman to his fingertips, a hard boss, but a fair one. He was a straight-dealing neighbour, too, adhering to the decencies which were required among the handful of ranchers attempting to survive on the desert-edge ranges.

Then old Sam died. He was a bachelor and had no kith or kin – or so the folk of Tinkettle Basin thought. They were wrong. It turned out there was an obscure relative, one Eli Brix, ranching up in Wyoming. It was doubtful whether old Sam really knew him or had even met him, but he left the S Bar B and everything else he owned to Brix. By that act, Sam Ballinger, who'd played squarely with his neighbours for decades, unwittingly dealt them the dirtiest of blows.

Eli Brix hit Tinkettle Basin like a tornado. He relocated from Wyoming, bringing down his hands and his herd to join the S Bar B stock and overcrowd the sparse ranges. He fired old Sam's retainers and renamed the outfit the Slanted B. It was rumoured that Brix and his riders had been involved in the Wyoming grass wars and the bunkhouse of his newly acquired outfit was now crammed with a decidedly unsavoury crew.

Old Lars shook his head despairingly as he recalled how rapidly things in Tinkettle Basin went downhill once Brix began to show his grasping hand.

Lars's old friend, Mark Clennan, was the first to feel the weight of the newcomer's presence with a blatant example of water-rustling. His pastures were nourished by a tributary of Tinkettle Creek, which gave life to the whole of the basin. For years, this tributary was shared amicably by Clennan's outfit and his neighbour, now styled the Slanted B. Finding that its waters had dwindled, though weather conditions were obviously not responsible, Mark Clennan took the risky step of venturing on to Brix's holdings to investigate. He did so alone because if he took any of his small crew or his three sons, the Slanted B riders might run them off with gunfire, claiming their lands were invaded.

Lars Lundgren knew what Mark Clennan found because Clennan told him the last time they met. The water had been deliberately dammed, plainly because Brix was out to maintain his overblown herd by stealing water from the MC.

Mark Clennan told Lars that he aimed to ride over to Brix's headquarters and have the matter out with him, even threatening legal action if he had to. Again, he proposed to do it alone, not wanting his sons or his men involved. Presumably that was what he did. No one knew what took place between the two ranchers, but within a week of

Mark Clennan's last conversation with Lars he was gunned down mercilessly in the main street of Brimstone by three masked men who emerged on foot from an alley, fired a hail of bullets then bolted back into the alley to retrieve their tethered horses and speed away. They disappeared even as bystanders were gasping in horror.

'But everyone knew Brix ordered it and Brix's men did it,' grunted Lars to himself. 'And, already, Brix had that damnfool Marshal Wiseman under his thumb. There was no proper investigation.'

He turned and entered his cabin, took his Winchester from its rack on the wall, inspected its action and nodded with satisfaction. He went to a drawer and produced his old Navy Colt, a faithful relic of his wild days in Montana. He set the chambers spinning and muttered that the weapon could stand a little oil.

He thought again of all that had passed since Eli Brix and his crew of hardcases came into Tinkettle Basin. Since the killing of Mark Clennan, his two older sons were slaughtered as unceremoniously as their father; the Clennan ranch went into Brix's hands and Brix extended his grasp over the bulk of the basin. And now the last of the Clennans had returned, bearing the brand of a killer, sporting the style of a gunfighter and dodging the tenacious Trillings who had trailed dozens of men throughout the West and hauled many off to the gallows.

Though Lew Clennan kept a tight lid on his emotions, he was plainly burning with an urge for vengeance and had plans which he would not divulge even to one so trusted as old Lars Lundgren.

'He's shown up like a summer thundercloud,' commented Lars to himself. 'Thunderclouds always burst and folks in these parts had better look to their weapons.'

Then he went off to check his supply of ammunition.

Lew Clennan rode the ridge trail cautiously, hunched forward in the saddle, attempting as far as possible not to skyline himself so that he could be spotted from the basin which spread below him with the thread of Tinkettle Creek running through it. The land he could see down there was once McClennan land where his father, his brothers, a hardworking crew and he himself had sweated to keep the MC outfit a going proposition. Now, the spread was under Eli Brix's Slanted B brand.

'A brand as crooked as it looks,' muttered Clennan to his mount bitterly.

His eyes swept the range, taking in groups of stock made tiny by distance and moving in grazing groups. He looked over to the east, saw the stone-studded rise of mountainous terrain and squinted to make out a barely discernible clutter of what might have been buildings or the remnants of them.

Scrunching his eyes against the glare of the climbing sun, he considered the distant vista of rising land. Riding this high ridge trail, cluttered by sun-split rocks and tall saguaro cactus called for cautious progress, but he considered that he would reach the abandoned settlement in perhaps an hour and reaching what was left of Kimmins City was part of his plan.

Clennan turned his horse around an outcrop of weather-sculptured rock where the trail took a sudden downward dip, and became abruptly alert as he heard the jingle of ringbits and the snort of horses. He was riding almost into the faces of a pair of horsemen coming from the opposite direction and just cresting the slope of the trail.

Both were young but with mean, hard and, sunburned faces under their sombreros. Clennan's gunman's instincts made him immediately glance at their belts. Each wore a Colt at his right side and the right hand of each automatically dropped to hover close to the butt of his weapon.

Hardcases! he thought. Then he remembered the reward dodger which had so mysteriously appeared here in Tinkettle Basin. Maybe these were Trilling agents, possibly it was they who were responsible for nailing the poster to the tree – and who knew how many more such posters to more trees?

One of the pair, bulkier than his companion, prodded his horse forward and halted it facing Clennan. In doing so the animal twisted its body slightly, so that Clennan caught sight of its brand – the Slanted B.

'What're you doing here, mister?' asked the

19

rider in a flat, grating voice. 'This is Slanted B land. You're trespassing.'

'This is not Slanted B land,' said Clennan. 'It never was unless the Slanted B has taken over the whole of the United States. This is public land and anyone can travel over it.'

At once, he felt he could have bitten out his tongue. The statement could well have been a mistake. With this pair, it might have been better to play the ignorant saddle tramp who did not know this country. They were not part of the Slanted B crew he had encountered before his departure from the basin and they did not know him. But now he had shown familiarity with the locality. It could focus the attention of Eli Brix and his outfit on him.

They faced each other for a moment of mounting tension, the two Slanted B riders taking his measure, each grasping his rein in his left hand, each with his right hand ominously close to the butt of his six-gun, ready to claw it.

Shadowed by his hat-brim, Lew Clennan's eyes were calm, telegraphing nothing to the pair. It would be two guns against one if it came to trouble and he did not want gunplay up here on the high ridge. Shots would echo across the rangeland below like clattering thunder, alerting any other Slanted B men. He would have to play it coolly and cleverly if he was going to get out of this situation with a whole skin and to his best advantage.

These two were young, obviously no choirboys but probably inexperienced for all that. He tried to imagine what was ticking away under their hats. Probably each was attempting to figure who he was, this newcomer who appeared to know something about where Slanted B boundaries began and ended. Possibly one or the other felt he might just be someone acquainted with their boss, Eli Brix, on his way to visit the Slanted B. They had good cause to fear Brix and to antagonize any friend of his would be unwise.

After a spell of silent stand-off, the less bulky of the pair displayed a jittery style. His hand twitched a little nearer his holster. Maybe he was the kind who liked to push for a fight – the kind who could start the very shooting-trouble Clennan did not want.

Clennan sat totally calm, his hands holding his reins and showing no sign of matching the trigger-itchiness of this pair who blocked his path and held two guns against his one. Youthful they might be but they were in a position make a play which could leave him dead.

And he knew it was time to break the impasse by forcing his own play.

CHAPTER TWO

TROUBLE IN HIS BACKTRAIL

Almost conversationally, Clennan asked: 'What're you two doing up here on the ridge, anyway?'

The heftier of the two Slanted B men curled his lip and said belligerently: 'Keeping undesirables away. Safeguarding Slanted B's interests, that's what.'

'Can't say you're making such a good job of it,' responded Clennan, jerking his head towards the panorama of graze land below. 'Looks like you haven't even noticed the signs of that grass fire beginning down yonder by the creek. It'll be a hell of a blaze in about ten minutes.'

Immediately the pair swung their heads to look down into the basin, seeking a non-existent grass fire. They never saw any movement from Lew Clennan's hands but when they switched their gaze back to him, they were looking into the mouth of his drawn Colt .45.

'Hoist your paws,' commanded Clennan. 'C'mon – hands in the air.'

With their jaws dropped in surprise, the two raised their hands.

'What the hell are you doing?' jittered the smaller of the two.

'Safeguarding *my* interests. Now, the two of you, lower your hands slowly and take off your gunbelts. Make the slightest move for your irons and I'll let daylight into you. I don't mind leaving a couple of meals for the buzzards up here.'

Visibly shaken, the Slanted B riders complied until each was holding his gunbelt, adorned by its holstered weapon.

'Now, pitch them down the ridge, guns, belts and all,' commanded Clennan harshly with a motion of his head towards the steep, rocky slope which descended from the edge of the ridge trail.

'*What?*' exploded the larger of the pair indignantly. 'You can't do this to us.'

'I *am* doing it to you. Now sling those belts and guns down the ridge and make sure you throw them well away from the trail.'

The Slanted B men complied, each hurling his belt and weapon over the rim of the ridge, then turning glowering faces to Lew Clennan while keeping their hands in the air.

'Lower your hands. Come down from your horses, do it slowly and don't try any smart moves or I'll ventilate the pair of you,' said Clennan.

The two climbed out of their saddles and stood sheepishly beside their animals while Clennan kept his Colt levelled unwaveringly at them.

'Now, take off your saddles. C'mon – take them clean off your cayuses.'

The Slanted B men glowered at him again, bewildered by the unusual order.

'C'mon – move!' snarled Clennan. The two set about unbuckling their saddle trappings, then each lifted his saddle from his horse.

'March to the edge of the trail and sling your saddles after your guns,' ordered Clennan. 'Go on – sling them well down the ridge and no half-measures!'

Again, the Slanted B riders complied, sending their saddles skittering down the sandy shale of the ridge, stirring up puffs of dust.

Lew Clennan grinned, spurred his bronc ahead and brushed past the two horses of the humiliated Slanted B men. '*Adios*, gents,' he called. 'Now go down the ridge and search for your guns and saddles.'

'By God, mister, we'll meet you again and we'll—' the slighter of the two howled, but his companion silenced him with a nudge to his arm. The unpredictable stranger had the drop on them and he could yet turn his gun on them and, as threatened, make them into buzzard-feed.

Clennan continued along the trail with a feeling of satisfaction. There was no chance of immediate pursuit by the pair. They would be too busy searching for their weapons and saddles and returning their saddles to their horses. He had already noted that they did not carry scabbarded rifles at their saddless, so they could not send any shots after him as he departed for their only firearms were lying somewhere down the sloping ridge.

'They'll be kept good and busy for quite a spell yet awhile,' Clennan remarked to the dun bronc.

His animal, burdened by travelling gear of war sack and blankets as well as rider, was wearying and when Clennan reached a small waterfall spilling down from the higher, rocky reaches of the ridge which towered over the trail, he stopped to allow it to drink and take a breather.

He sat on a rock and got to thinking.

Dammit – maybe that move with the Slanted B men was not so smart after all.

He'd derived much satisfaction from it, sure, but it had certainly drawn attention to his presence in Tinkettle Basin where it might have been better to keep his head down for a spell. There was that puzzling matter of the Trilling Detective Agency's reward poster – and possibly more of them – appearing in this country. When word got around about the incident on the ridge trail, Brix and his Slanted B crew, alerted by the poster, might only too easily conclude that it was the last of the Clennans who was responsible.

That thought was countered by a reflection on the likely reaction of the Slanted B pair. Youngsters who had ambitions of fitting in with the hardcases on Eli Brix's payroll were more likely to keep as tight-mouthed as clams about the stranger who had made fools of them on the ridge trail. They would not want to endure the guffaws of the bunkhouse that would be sure to greet any admission of being deprived of their guns and saddles by a lone gunman and being made to scrabble in the shale of the ridge slopes to retrieve them.

'I'll bet that, even now, one is telling the other to keep his mouth firmly shut when they get back to the Slanted B,' he told the drinking bronc with satisfaction.

Even so, though the incident with the two riders had avoided any shooting which would have alerted the Slanted B, he wondered whether he might have handled the matter differently. Indeed, the whole incident might have been an indication of a disturbing reversion to the old impetuosity which had characterized his young days here in Tinkettle Basin. That tendency to act on the spur of the moment, taking the speediest solution which suggested itself, was something he ought to have left behind him long ago.

It was his ever rash frame of mind that had set him against his two brothers and led to his leaving the basin in the first place. In the wake of their father's murder, Frank and Ed spoke of legal means of redress but that was more easily considered than accomplished in this back-of-beyond section of Arizona Territory. The marshal of Brimstone was no paragon as a lawman to start with, and he soon showed signs of becoming too cosy with Eli Brix as soon as Brix began spreading his money around. The town's only lawyer, Horace

Tait, was a drunk, just about capable of rudimentary transactions and no courtroom crusader for justice. While Frank and Ed, gifted with their father's balanced good sense, tried to find a proper solution to the mystery of Mark Clennan's killing, a couple of the best hands on their small MC spread gave in to cold feet and quit. The third brother became more impatient.

He was for decisive action against Brix and his hard-bitten crew. He wanted to fight.

'Brix is aiming to grab land,' he bellowed during one of the long arguments between the brothers. 'He started with water-rustling and now he's gone on to murder our old man. He aims to dominate the basin. Before the few small ranchers here are bullied off their holdings, we should all get together and fight him.'

'I suppose you mean ride against him and shoot it out with his crew,' Frank had roared back at him. 'We can't do that.'

'Why not? There's no effective law in the basin. We'll have to stand up for ourselves. Nobody else will do it for us.'

Ed pitched in. 'That would be vigilante action. It's against the law,' he protested. 'We'd set off a range war like they had in Montana and Wyoming. We don't want that kind of bloodshed here.'

'Well, Wyoming is where Brix and his bunch came from and the talk is that they were involved in the grass wars up there. They're experienced at the game and if we used our brains, we'd pool our resources and strike at the Slanted B before Brix really gets his teeth into the basin. I say things have gone far enough!' hooted Lew.

'That's just damfool, hot-headed talk,' Frank objected. 'The old man worked hard to build this place out of nothing. He and our mother struggled to make it worth having. The old man wasn't scared of a fight but he respected the law, even if there was little of it, and he was all for peace. He wouldn't want us and our neighbours to set off a graze war in Tinkettle Basin.'

'Hell, even the old man knew when enough was enough and he was near the end of his tether with the water-rustling move,' growled Lew. 'I reckon he was just about ready for a fight. I don't know what he said to Brix when he met him, but I figure he made war talk which got Brix's dander up.'

The wrangles between the three brothers continued for days with Frank and Ed showing the thoughtful restraint inherited from their father while Lew persisted in stubbornly pushing for a fighting resolution to the troubles overshadowing the basin. His tempestuousness was a legacy from his mother, the spirited and determined beauty who had been the resourceful and courageous partner in Mark Clennan's efforts to carve a ranch out of a portion of Tinkettle Basi. She was carried away by fever soon after Lew was born.

The elder brothers saw an approach to the US marshal in Tucson as a way of redressing the gunning down of their father, since they had no faith in the law in Brimstone, the basin's only town. Lew was scornful. 'That means the politicians will stick their noses in,' he objected. 'People who aspire to the kind of power Eli Brix is looking for always square politicians who'll help them and I'll bet he's got his connections among the gang in Tucson. They're plumb sure to interfere. There's an old-fashioned way of settling land fights in Arizona – and you know what it is!'

'And we don't want any of it,' responded Frank forcibly. 'One killing in the basin is enough. I have faith in the integrity of the federal law and I say we take it up with the US marshal. That'd be the legal thing to do.'

In the face of their unwavering stonewalling, Lew lost all patience and, one night, packed his war sack, saddled up and rode out while his brothers were sleeping.

'I was a blasted fool,' he told the horse as it finished drinking beside the ridge trail. 'I let Frank and Ed down when I should have stood by them. Maybe I was even loco half the time. The old man's death hit me harder than maybe I could admit. Still, I should have stayed instead of hazing off and getting myself into a hell of a lot of trouble elsewhere.'

He took the reins and led the animal away from the natural rock sink into which the waterfall tumbled. 'Still, I'm back now – and Eli Brix and the Slanted B are going to know it!'

Another twenty minutes' travel along the trail brought him to a point where he could look down upon the basin's pastures from a new angle. He saw the clutter of buildings along the width of the main street of Brimstone and, off in the middle distance, the sketchy suggestion of a house with ill-defined shapes of corrals in its yard. His eyes dwelt on it and a lump rose in his throat. It was the headquarters of the MC outfit. It didn't look much from this distance, but it was the place his father had struggled to establish; it was where he was born and was raised. It was from there that he had stormed out in his rage against his brothers.

Then, hard upon the thoughts of Frank and Ed came the aching memory of how he heard of subsequent events.

He'd taken up with a Texas cattle-drive through the Indian Nations. In mid-drive, his crew had met up with a set of riders making the return after disposing of their herd at the Kansas railhead. The two sets of wranglers mingled to share coffee, smokes and news of the outside world. One of the chance-met trail companions turned out to be a young fellow from the Tinkettle Basin locality.

'I sure was sorry to hear about Frank and Ed,' he told Lew Clennan. 'Got word of it in a letter from my old man just before my outfit left on the drive. He said folks around the basin are blaming Eli Brix and his bunch. I reckon they're not far wrong. He's getting powerful big in the basin.'

Clennan caught his breath. 'Frank and Ed? Why, what's wrong?'

The young fellow looked at him incredulously. 'You mean you don't know?' he asked huskily. 'Hell, they were both killed. Bushwhacked. Waylaid on the stretch of trail that goes through

30

the wooded country between Brimstone and your place. It's plain as day that they were ambushed from the cover of the trees but it's all a mystery as far as the law in Brimstone is concerned – but you know the quality of the law in Brimstone.'

Clennan was gripped by mingled shock and anger and the breath gusted out of him. Frank and Ed murdered, and the hand of Eli Brix was seen in it! And this had happened after he stormed off the MC ranch, when he should have been there to back up his brothers in the face of the land-grabbing menace which all too obviously loomed over the Tinkettle Basin ranges.

When he found his voice he asked his informant why his brothers were riding in the wooded region where the bushwhacking took place.

'Well, according to my old man's letter, they were returning from Brimstone. Talk is that they'd been to Horace Tait's office, negotiating papers for the sale of the MC to Brix. At least, that's what's said around the basin and, sure enough, your old family outfit is now owned by Brix. Slanted B beef is running on what was MC land.'

'What?' Clennan bellowed. After word of his brothers' deaths, this news was a second hammerblow. 'If Brix has his hands on our outfit, it was done by trickery. I'm damned sure Frank and Ed would never make it over through a legal sale. Even if they ever considered it, they'd never deal with that drunken oaf Horace Tait. Anyway, I have a share in that property through my old man's will and they would never sell without consulting me. If this was an above-board deal, they would have tracked me down.'

His first reaction was to quit the drive at once, head back to Tinkettle Basin and go gunning for Eli Brix and the whole Slanted B outfit. But he had signed on to wrangle the herd up to Kansas and the crew was already short-handed. A core of logic in the maelstrom of anger within him told him he needed time to settle down and think coolly. Seething with pent-up fury, he calmed his impetuosity and went through the drive with dark thoughts of vengeance. He made a prickly companion throughout the trip and return – a tetchy man who was handy with a gun and carried a cargo of deep grievance.

A man in such a mood was almost sure to find trouble and Lew Clennan found it when the trail crew made its return to Purple Flats, a Texas town largely run by a cattle and land company. After being paid off, the most pressing matter on his mind was a speedy return to Arizona and Tinkettle Basin. He wanted to know the truth about his brothers' murders. He wanted to know how the MC lands went into Eli Brix's hands. And, nagging at his innards was a desire for vengeance because he knew there had been criminality at Tinkettle Basin where, he was sure, an already inept version of law and order had been twisted in favour of Brix, the man who was trying to rule the locality.

He stopped off for a final drink with the trail wranglers and, in the saloon, he was noted by a swaggering and truculent youngster, packing a pair of Colt .45s, a youth with half-mad eyes who was plainly looking for a ruckus. His smouldering gaze lighted on Clennan and, with something like eager relish, on the six-gun holstered at his hip.

The cowpuncher standing next to Clennan at the bar whispered hastily: 'Watch out for this guy. I know him and he's loco. He's trying to build a reputation and you have the look of a gunslinger. He'll try to bait you.' With that the wrangler slipped away to make himself scarce.

Lew Clennan took in the two sixshooters sported by this youngster whose powderkeg disposition clearly matched his own. It was going to be two guns against his one – and there was no doubt that a fight was coming.

His trail companions speedily left their drinks on the bar and melted into the background. The reputation-seeker marched boldly up to Clennan, glowered into his face, drew back his lips in a snarl and offered an insult.

'*Back your foul mouth!*' snarled Clennan.

The young troublemaker was fast. Both of his guns were clear of leather when Clennan's speedier Colt came up and blasted a bullet through his heart.

The young gunslinger's twin weapons clattered on the boards. His eyes went blank, his mouth dropped open and he pitched face forward through a wreath of gunsmoke like a felled tree.

There was a moment of total stillness, then Lew

Clennan heard the foreman of his crew of drovers yell: 'It was fair and square! He drew on Lew first! It was self-defence!'

Another voice sounded: 'Hell! That was Tom Langler! His old man's a boss of the company. There'll be hell to pay for this!'

Clennan stood frozen to the spot. He was always a hot-head and he knew it, and he could handle a gun. He'd proved himself as a marksman many times but he had never before killed a man.

Even before he overcame his moment of shock, the batwing doors of the saloon burst open. A paunchy man with a star on his vest strode in, followed by two more similarly adorned. All were carrying shotguns.

'What's going on in here? What was that shooting about?' demanded the marshal of Purple Flats. His eyes widened when he looked at the body lying face down in front of the bar, then at Lew Clennan, still grasping his Colt with a thread of smoke dribbling form its mouth.

'Damn it – that's Bob Langler's son,' he gasped. 'Looks like you've killed him, mister, and this town will make you pay a big price.' With his deputies in his wake, he walked up to Clennan and shoved his shotgun into his midriff. 'Hand over that gun. You're under arrest,' he stated. The statement was given emphasis by each deputy simultaneously cocking a round into his shotgun.

A silent knot of trail crew and saloon patrons watched as Clennan handed his gun to the law officer. The lawmen crowded in on him and marched him towards the door.

He was escorted across the street towards an adobe building which bore a sign indicating that it was the town marshal's office and jail. He saw his horse, tethered with those of the trail crew at the hitch rack outside the saloon and, as the chill shock of the shooting eased, he began to calculate his chances of running for the animal, mounting and riding out fast. But, with the trio of determined law officers in such close attendance, he knew it was a forlorn hope.

He was pushed into the narrow street doorway of the jail and, just as the party was under the lintel, his chance suddenly arose.

The men were in such close proximity in the confined space that Clennan realized that one of the deputies was crammed hard against him, his holstered revolver brushing against Clennan's hip. Clennan grabbed the weapon, snatched it from its leather and, at the same time, slammed his boot down on the deputy's foot. The man gave a howl and dropped his shotgun. Somebody tried to grasp Clennan but he wriggled and lashed out with his foot, finding a shin with a severe kick which brought forth another howl.

Arms flailed and the lawmen were falling over each other in the narrow passageway.

Clutching the deputy's six-gun, Clennan bolted for the street and his tethered animal. He was halfway across the street's rutted expanse before the trio of lawmen came spilling out on to the boardwalk. A panicky and badly aimed shotgun shell *whanged* over his head. He ducked, turned and fired back a random shot. It zipped past the ear of the Marshal, a circumstance which the subsequent reward dodgers would pump up into a claim of attempted murder.

As Clennan reached the hitch rack, he heard one of the deputies yell hoarsely: 'I'll get him, Marshal!'

Then the marshal roared: 'Don't shoot, you blamed fool! There are citizens on the street. I don't want innocent people hurt!'

Townsfolk were running for cover and the confusion and the respite in the firing gave Clennan a chance to unhitch his rein and swing into the saddle. He rowelled the horse's flanks and split the wind for the end of the street. He knew a posse would be raised and he had the disadvantage of being in country he scarcely knew, but he had a good start and his mount was spirited and energetic.

Outside town he found tangled territory of mesquite-dotted ridges and dried watercourses, good country for a rider to lose himself in so long as he was not too closely pursued. He was guided more by instinct than by accurate knowledge but he believed he was riding in the general direction of the band of hardly settled territory known as the Cherokee Strip, bordering northern Texas. His hope was that the jurisdiction of the lawmen from Purple Flats petered out somewhere around the Texas line.

He was well into a labyrinth of humped land and

gullies by the time night had fully fallen and it was evident that he had outwitted any pursuers. It was unthinkable that a party from Purple Flats had not set out after him but he must have lost them in this confusing terrain. He made a wary night-camp beside a small stream between shoulders of land where there was sufficient grazing for his horse and pressed on before dawn. He found he had crossed the line into the Cherokee Strip when he came across a small encampment of Osage Indians who were out hunting. They shared a meal with him, sold him some strips of beef jerky and indicated the way to New Mexico.

Clennan made a hard wayfaring there and, in a raw, one-street town, chanced a night in what passed as a hotel. This gave him an opportunity to rest his horse and provide it with some substantial feed. His luck held, for it seemed word of the happenings in Purple Flats had not filtered through to New Mexico. In the morning he embarked on a cautious traversing of New Mexico's largely desert miles and eventually emerged in Arizona.

Now, this prodigal with trouble – and the Trilling Detective Agency – in his backtrail was on the ridge-trail in familiar land. He looked down into the basin and on to the spread which he knew had been inveigled out of the ownership of his brothers and himself. He remembered the surge of bitterness he had experienced when the chance-met wrangler on the trail told him of the killing of Frank and Ed; how Lars Lundgren had taken care of their funerals and how Eli Brix had forced others off the Tinkettle Basin ranges.

The old, gnawing remorse which he knew only too well returned when he thought of how he had left his brothers. He tried to find excuses for it. Perhaps he was too slow in growing up and leaving behind his petulance and his hot-headedness; perhaps he was even slightly unbalanced by the bushwhacking of his father. At all events, he should have remained in the basin to support Frank and Ed and stand against the Slanted B. If he'd listened to their sober assessments, the three of them might have formed a workable leadership to scotch Brix's land-grabbing. As things were now turning out, Eli Brix was on the way to driving all the decent kind, people like Lars and the neighbours he had known all his life, off these ranges and stamping the Slanted B brand on the whole of Tinkettle Basin.

'Not if I can stop it,' he muttered to his mount. 'I was a damned fool and I owe a debt to Frank and Ed. But I'm back now. I have a fair poke of money in the Brimstone bank, saved since I was a kid, to back my play and I have a claim on the MC land until someone shows me a paper recording a legal sale and hands me my rightful share from it. I'm damned sure no such paper exists. I'm back with scores to settle and Eli Brix will find I'm prodding for trouble.'

He took a last look down into the vistas of Tinkettle Basin, his eyes resting on the distant headquarters of his family's ranch. His mouth tightened into a dogged line and he urged his horse forward, heading for the frowning uplands above the basin and, in particular, for the ghost town of Kimmins City.

CHAPTER THREE

GHOST TOWN

Kimmins City was grandly named but, even in its
best days, it had never amounted to much.
Founded by Old Man Kimmins on what looked
like the site of a substantial strike, it once had
ambitions towards becoming a substantial mining
town. The strike, however, was a freak rather than
proof of a rich seam running under the rocky
escarpment on which the settlement mush-
roomed, and it died as speedily as the town came
into being. Overnight, the miners and the avaricious chancers who followed in their wake – the
gamblers, the saloon-keepers, the dance-hall
promoters and their attendant ladies – disappeared.

They left a huddle of warped, weather-wrecked
wooden shacks and adobe brick hovels. These
were arranged higgledy-piggledy alongside an ill-
defined track which once passed for a street and

40

was now throttled by wind-blown sand and shale, clogged by cactus and catclaw and roamed by tumbleweeds. It was eerily silent, sweltering in the sun and its ruins held the threat of scorpions and rattlesnakes.

The ghost town offered nothing in the way of attractions except one that was of paramount importance to Lew Clennan – its ragged remnant of the street petered out at the very edge of the escarpment which frowned over Tinkettle Basin.

It was towards this point that Clennan rode. He had known Kimmins City since his boyhood. It had lost its reason for existence in his earliest youth and, as a kid who loved ranging far and wide on a pony, he found its decayed ruins suggestive of adventure. Riding up the ragged remains of the street, he saw, as he had expected, that everything had deteriorated yet more since his last visit. Dried-out timber and old adobe bricks crumbled in the heat and, in the still air, even the numerous tumbleweeds were motionless. It seemed perhaps aeons since any human had set foot in this place, once a manifestation of the brashness of man but now almost wholly reclaimed by savage nature.

Clennan wondered whether, as in the past, the occasional saddle tramp or wandering Indian still found their way here to make temporary camp. The attraction for those who knew the country was the small rill, fed by a natural spring and running to one side of the street. In the days when the place attempted to be a town it was ringed around by bricks and kept as a public water supply for human and beast.

He allowed the bronc to pick its way over the uncertain surface of the forlorn street and reached the point where it finished on the edge of the elevated land overlooking Tinkettle Basin. He halted the animal and considered the sweep of the landscape below.

Any military commander would have recognized this point as a superb high-ground position. Tinkettle Creek and the fertile expanse of its basin flattened away into the heat-hazed distance beyond which lay Mexico. A smudge of blue chimney smoke marked the town of Brimstone and the northern regions of the land once grazed over by MC stock and now in the hands of Eli Brix were discernible.

There was only one major horseback route up here from the basin and that was by way of the ridge trail Clennan had just travelled. It could be seen, snaking along the shoulder of high land to one side of the basin. A sniper planted at the point he now occupied could pick off anyone on the trail as they approached.

He noted with satisfaction that the trail was empty. Obviously, the two Slanted B men had not thought fit to take off in pursuit of him. Probably, they had been so hard put to it, scrabbling on slopes of the ridge in search of their saddles and guns as well as taking time to resaddle their mounts that he simply had too good a start on them. He pulled his mouth into a doubtful smile. His action against the pair was a good trick at the time and it had given him much satisfaction, but it could alert the Slanted B to his presence in the locality. The men were not part of Eli Brix's original crew, who would have recognized Clennan on sight, and the crude portrait on the Trillings' reward poster was unlikely to have given them a clue as to his identity. Nevertheless, word would surely get around that a gun-toting upstart had shown up.

'I can expect trouble from down yonder in the basin sooner or later,' he growled to himself. 'My hope is that I can be smart enough to dab Eli Brix in the eye first – and do it in spades!'

He turned the bronc and angled it down the remains of the street again, trying to remember just where the water supply was located and hoping it had not dried up over the years. He found it behind a gap between two humps of tumbled boards which had once been buildings. It still ran fresh, feeding a pool contained between the remnants of old adobe bricks. There was even a flourishing of grass around the spot, making it a miniature oasis in the desert surroundings. This was welcome feed for the bronc and Clennan dismounted to allow the animal to graze.

He drank, found the water fresh, then led the animal to the pool and watched it slaking its thirst, ensuring that it did not consume too much. A buzz of flies attracted his attention and an investigation of a hump of ground close by revealed a deposit of horse-droppings certainly less than twenty-four hours old.

Clennan walked slowly around the site, examining the ground and found trampled tracks leading from the street, then back again to be lost in the unreadable drifts of sand and shale. They clearly suggested two animals, one smaller-hoofed than the other and probably a mule. The spot had been visited by some wanderer, packing enough freight to require an animal of burden. Possibly it was a prospector, hopeful of making a strike in this region of Old Man Kimmins's long-failed bonanza.

Whoever it was had visited the place very recently and might still be somewhere in the vicinity. Clennan stood in the dust of the street, looking cautiously around. There was only stillness without the slightest breath of a breeze. He planned to hole up here on the unpopulated tableland over Tinkettle Basin, clear of the basin itself but within reach of it and with a commanding view of the approaches which gave him a chance of holding off anyone who came in search of him.

The last thing he wanted was to share his isolated hideaway with anyone who had similar intentions of making a permanent camp there.

A sudden, startling sound disturbed him from somewhere behind – the sharp, unmistakable double click of a Winchester rifle being pumped.

He whirled, his hand grabbing for the butt of his holstered Colt. Behind him, there was nothing but the empty, sand-drifted straggle of the street with its dried-out ruins, mouldering in the still, heavy air. Yet he was absolutely sure he had heard the sound of a weapon being pumped.

44

A slight, eerie wind whipped up small whorls of dust along the deserted street but there was otherwise no sign of movement. Clennan looked around, seeing only the silent, crumbled adobe brick and the warped, false-fronted wooden structures of this decayed place.

He shrugged, thinking that the recent strains of being on the dodge and his sustained hard riding were causing his nerves to play tricks. Maybe he had imagined the sound of a pump-action weapon being cocked. Then he recalled how, at the source of water he had found plain signs of someone having been there recently. Did someone still lurk among the ruins of the town – someone armed with a rifle who might ambush him from concealment at any moment? He tried to dismiss his suspicions, telling himself that he was merely giving in to the jitters. But the memories of the bushwhackings of his father and brothers came surging back, bringing shuddering, icy unease.

He kept his hand on the butt of his six-gun, scoured both sides of the street with his eyes, came close to calling out for the concealed personage to show himself, then realized that he was probably being foolish. He was getting to be like some old desert rat who was half-crazy through spending too long in the solitary wilderness – and derelict Kimmins City was just the place to cause a man's grip on his reason to slip.

He tried to still his anxiety. There *had* been someone with a horse and a pack-mule here lately, but it was surely some desert wanderer, maybe one of the hopeful prospectors, ever seeking a strike. As for the sound of a weapon being cocked, that was surely only a trick of the wind or the scuttling of some jackrabbit or gila monster among the dried-out ruins.

He went about doing what he had to do here in Kimmins City, but he kept his hand close to his holster. For he was dogged by the notion that there were eyes on him in this haunted place.

Clay Reeder and Slip Corkery had been disgruntled ever since arriving in Arizona. They chafed under the heat of a brassy sun beating from a cloudless sky, and were irritated by the dust and sweat of hours on horseback, following trails through an arid terrain which seemed never-ending. It was all enough to weary the most intrepid of travellers but Reeder and Corkery were no quitters. They were here to do a job and they were determined to do it, riding doggedly onward and enduring the discomfort in silence.

They had hunted men through all quarters of the West: on the high plains of Montana, Wyoming and the Dakotas; through the dune country of Nebraska and the flats of the Indian Nations. They had searched the course of the Columbia River, nudging the Canadian border and the hard-scrabble lands along the Rio Grande in Texas. And both preferred to be anywhere but traversing the parched map of the south-west, penetrating the scrub and deserts of Arizona and New Mexico.

Mounted on gaunt steeds with travel gear

stacked behind their saddles, they made a discon-
certing pair at whom residents of the small towns
through which they passed and travellers encountered on the trail looked askance. When they
stopped off for grub or to slake their thirsts in
ramshackle saloons and cantinas, the other
customers instinctively clammed up and drew away
from them. Nothing about this pair invited
amiable conversation and the Colt revolvers
holstered at their hips and the Henry rifles which
they invariably lifted from their saddle scabbards
and carried when they entered matched their
edgy, watchful caution.

Both wore black, broad-brimmed sombreros
and long, grubby duster coats over nondescript
range garb. They looked dangerous from their
battered headgear to their cut-down Texas boots
with big-rowelled spurs.

Clay Reeder was tall and skinny with a high beak
of a nose set in a melancholy face, deeply etched
by experience and scarred by savage suns.

Slip Corkery was shorter but hardly plumper
and most of the lower portion of his face was
hidden by a huge and mournful walrus moustache.
There was no suggestion of sunny dispositions,
light-heartedness or humour about this pair. They
were ever deadly serious and they carried out their
business with a gravity becoming to undertakers
which, in a way, was what they were. For Reeder
and Corkery were man-trackers and the men they
tracked and caught frequently expired at the end
of a hangman's rope. They were bounty hunters,

who went in search of rewards. At present they could call themselves agents of the Trilling Detective Agency and they carried printed cards to prove it. But they were still bounty hunters.

And the man they hunted here in Arizona was Lew Clennan.

They rode a dusty trail, guarded by sun-split rocks and tall saguaro cactus and snaking over flat desert lands dotted with clumps of scrub and Joshua trees.

Breaking a silence of the better part of an hour, Slip Corkery said through his walrus moustache: 'How far is this damned Tinkettle Basin place?'

'Somewhere ahead, like every place in this blamed, dried-up territory,' answered his companion. 'Everywhere is somewhere ahead and it's always too blasted far away.'

'D'you figure we'll find Clennan there?' asked Corkery.

'He might be there, maybe in the jail of this Marshal Wiseman, if Wiseman has acted on the information sent by the agency and arrested him or, if he ever was there, he might have skipped for the high hills because he saw those posters the agency was stupid enough to send out,' stated Clay Reeder in his colourless monotone. 'Sending reward dodgers was a damnfool idea. They'll just warn Clennan that we're on his tail. I like to sneak up on a man right out of nowhere and grab him.'

'Hell, he shot his way out of the Purple Flats jail. He might do the same thing in Brimstone. He's hell on wheels with a gun by all accounts,' said Corkery.

The notion that Clennan shot his way out of the Purple Flats jail was part of the myth already obscuring the truth of what happened in the Texas town and intensifying the portrayal of the wanted man as a ruthless desperado. Reeder and Corkery had hunted men as freelances for years, lured by the rewards offered by federal, municipal or private law-enforcement agencies such as the Trilling Detective Agency. They had, this late in their careers, managed to secure places on the Trilling payroll which meant, in the present instance, that they could reap a double benefit – a salary from the company boosted by the $500 reward on Clennan's head to be split between them. This last glittering prize, however, depended on their capturing him before someone else who would thereby collect the booty. For all their complaining Reeder and Corkery were prepared to sweat in pursuit of the reward – and they were utterly determined to get it.

At this moment, however, their pursuit was engendering little else but sweat. Something like a positive start might be made once they found Brimstone and the office of its marshal, who might furnish something in the way of information as to the habits and resorts of Lew Clennan, known as a local resident. The trouble was, the pair seemed to be lost.

'Dammit, I get the notion we're riding in circles,' grunted Corkery thickly. 'I'm plumb sure we passed that same rock an hour ago.'

'We wouldn't be lost if I had my map of Arizona Territory,' responded Reeder testily. 'It was a damn good army map and you had to go and leave it in that last room we had in that fleabag hotel in Benson.'

'I never touched the map,' protested Corkery through his thick moustache. 'You had it the whole time. If it's lost then you lost it. And now we're stuck out in nowhere without even a jackrabbit in sight to give us directions.'

They rode on in strained silence for a spell, then noticed that the landscape was becoming fresher, with more evidence of greenery. The trail became elevated, surmounting a hump of terrain and, from the summit, Clay Reeder looked ahead, screwing his eyes to take in the distant vistas which appeared decidedly more fertile. He could make out corrals, penning in horses on a far splash of green grazing and with a sizable log house nearby.

'Looks like a horse ranch,' he reported. 'Might have something to do with that big rancher, Brix, we hear runs things around Tinkettle Basin. Might get a line on Clennan there.'

'And at least there's a chance to water and feed our cayuses and maybe find a cup of coffee if the people are friendly,' anticipated Corkery.

Lars Lundgren, standing in the yard fronting his cabin, watched the pair approach, and knew at once from their style and demeanour exactly what they were.

'*Trillings*!' He snorted. '*Looking for Lew without a*

doubt. Time for the dumb Swede to act.'

Reeder and Corkery rode in at a walk, stirring banners of dust and Reeder raised his hand in greeting.

'Howdy,' he called. 'We're looking for the town of Brimstone. Seems we got ourselves off the track somewhere.'

Lars trudged towards them, putting on a weary shuffle. He cupped his hand around his right ear. In a halting and exaggerated accent, he hooted: 'What – I'm deaf as all hell – ain't got much good English, neither! What you say, mister?'

'Brimstone!' bawled Reeder. 'We're looking for Brimstone.'

'You'll have to shout, mister,' replied Lars. 'What're you talking about?'

Corkery gave a frustrated grunt. 'He's a blamed Dutchman and deaf as a beetle. Seems we're striking nothing but hard luck in this country.'

Reeder tried again, almost bellowing himself hoarse. 'Brimstone! Where's Brimstone?'

'Oh, *ja* – Brimstone. Pretty damn lousy town! Out yonder.' He swept his arm in a wide gesture which took in most of the immediate portion of Arizona Territory and was of no practical use to Reeder and Corkery. 'You fellows want some coffee? Got water and feed for your horses around the side of the house, too – you help yourselves – *ja*.'

That at least was encouraging, and the man-hunters came down from their saddles wearily.

Lars Lundgren was thinking fast. If only he knew

where Lew Clennan was he might have some chance of getting word to him that this pair were in the vicinity. It occurred to him that he could send one of the two trustworthy Navajo youths who gave him a hand with the stock from time to time to seek him with a warning. But Clennan had stayed tight-mouthed as to his intentions and where he was headed after he left Lars's ranch. At least, Lars reasoned, he could delay this unsavoury-looking pair and make their lives uncomfortable.

Clay Reeder walked up to Lars and, from closer quarters, tried further shouted questioning.

'You ever hear of Lew Clennan?'

'What? What you say?'

'Clennan – Lew Clennan. Do you know him? Have you seen him?'

'Oh, *ja* – Lew Clennan. I seen him. Seen him, all right, many times – *ja*.'

Reeder and Corkery suddenly became attentive.

'When?' demanded Reeder. 'When did you see him?'

'And where?' put in Slip Corkery.

'Oh, years ago. When he was a kid. I knew his old man. Too bad his kid Lew left home, *ja* – turned into a gunman, I hear – been away for years.'

Reeder snorted and Corkery spat in to the dust in disgust.

'How about that coffee?' asked Lars disarmingly. 'I don't get many folks passing through. You're sure welcome to sit awhile. Rest your horses.'

Reeder and Corkery benefited from this visit to

the old Swede's horse ranch through the coffee, served with cold cuts of meat and bread which Lars provided and which they consumed while sitting in the shade of his porch, and through the water, feed and rest which refreshed their animals. But that was the only true satisfaction they had.

Just before they saddled up to ride off, the pair tried again to get precise directions to Brimstone. This time it was Corkery who bellowed the questions.

'Oh, *ja* – Brimstone,' said Lars. 'Go north, find the track with the black boulders – OK – *ja?* A short cut, that – two black boulders – *ja.*'

The pair nodded. At last, this sounded like positive advice.

'Take the trail by the two black boulders. Thanks, old-timer,' shouted Reeder, mounting up.

The Trilling agents rode off Lars's place with some feeling of satisfaction. They had obtained a measure of assistance from the old Swede but had very quickly wearied of trying to converse with him by bawling themselves hoarse. At least, they believed, he had set them on the road to Brimstone and it was essential that they sought out Marshal Wiseman and had access to a telegraph so they could contact the Trilling agency's headquarters in Austin, Texas. They had also rested, eaten, replenished their canteens and fed, watered and rubbed down their horses.

With mixed feelings, Lars Lundgren watched the dust in their backtrail dwindle. Helped by his pose as a deaf old coot with halting English, seemingly on the edge of his dotage, he had delayed them for a spell. He derived huge pleasure from the fact that the trail guarded by two black boulders was neither of the two trails which mattered hereabouts: the one leading into Tinkettle Basin, the Slanted B Ranch and the town of Brimstone and the ridge trail, which climbed up the high slant of terrain to the tableland beyond the fertile basin. The boulder-guarded trail was, in fact, a dim track which petered out on the fringe of parched alkali flats.

With a grin, Lars reflected that, by nightfall, the pair of Trilling men would be well and truly frustrated in the midst of nowhere and doubtless forced to make a dry night-camp. But they had the brand of tenacious trackers on them and it was unlikely that they would be long deterred from their task.

He still wished he could have somehow warned Lew Clennan of the arrival of the two man-hunters. But Clennan, keeping his own counsel, had disappeared to follow his own mysterious plans.

'And he sure has trouble with that pair on his trail, wherever he is,' rumbled Lars.

CHAPTER FOUR

HUNTING LEW CLENNAN

Daylight was fading over ruined Kimmins City as Lew Clennan walked cautiously along a partly rotted boardwalk, peering into one building after another. At last, near the end of the street, he found one which seemed to suit his purpose. It was the remains of a warped wooden store, still with a substantial roof. Its single large room appeared to be relatively clean and seemed not to be harbouring any nests of rattlers or rats.

It was not the last word in luxury but a man might pitch his bedroll there and make a form of headquarters out of it. For that was Clennan's intention. He meant to hole up here, out of Tinkettle Basin but near enough to it to make excursions there, although he knew they would be fraught with danger. This old store had the double advantage of being close to both the spring of water and to the end of the street, almost on the edge of the lip which overlooked the low-lying ranges of the basin. From there he had a clear view of the ridge trail, leading upwards. If need be, he could hold off with rifle fire any riders venturing up the trail well before they were within reach of Kimmins City – provided he was not taken by surprise in the night. And nights would surely prove hazardous once his enemies had wind of his being in the locality and if they pinpointed the ruined settlement as his hiding-place.

And when he thought of the night, he thought again of that sound of a rifle being cocked which he might or might not have heard on the haunted air of Kimmins City.

There were priorities to which he must give consideration before he set in motion his plans against Eli Brix, and those whom he believed were in league with him. He aimed to wage war against the man who was making himself the emperor of Tinkettle Basin – and a war required preparations. It was a lone-hand game and a big proposition but he had already formed a step-by-step plan of action.

He needed ammunition. The Colt in his holster was the one snatched from the deputy back in Purple Flats. It was, by a stroke of luck, the same pattern of .45 as his own pistol but he had only a limited amount of bullets in the shell-belt at his waist and he carried in his pack a mere modicum of ammunition for the Winchester in his saddle scabbard. In fact he was equipped with nothing more than the average working cowpuncher. Then there was food. If he was going to hole up in the eerie confines of Kimmins City for any length of time, he must have supplies.

His money was limited to the remains of his pay for the cattle-drive out of Texas. It had been a hard-earned, generous amount but, by this time, it had dwindled. He had money in a longstanding account at the Brimstone bank, down in Tinkettle Basin, and he intended to avail himself of it in due course. For now, however, he knew he must stretch out the limited amount he had as best he could.

The hinterland beyond Kimmins City existed as almost another world from the low-lying, fertile basin of Tinkettle Creek. It was a vast spread of tableland, flattening away towards a ragged skyline of buttes and mesas, fringing the drylands. It had desert-edge ranches, some more prosperous than others depending on the fickleness of the water supplies. Its folk usually went about their business oblivious to what was going on down in Tinkettle Basin. They had hard enough lives of their own to contend with.

The nearest town on this spread of tableland was Rock Crossing, a settlement as unlovely as Brimstone, which had sprouted on a minor creek. Clennan was certainly known there and he wondered if the Trilling Agency's lurid reward dodger had been circulated thereabouts. Even if it had, he reasoned, he could take some comfort from the fact that its portrait was so poor that he certainly would not be immediately recognized from it by someone who had never seen him in the flesh. At all events, he needed to replenish his resources and Rock Crossing was the nearest convenient place to do it. He would have to risk a visit.

He stood under the slanted lintel of the door of the old building and, in rapidly dying light, considered the contents of his billfold. He calculated that he had enough for a war sack full of food, a replenishment of ammunition and even a night in the town's somewhat woeful hotel in order to recover from the forced riding of recent days.

He contemplated leaving some of his travel gear in this building, selected as his hiding-place, but recalled the memory of that ghostly sound suggesting some other human presence here in Kimmins City and decided against it.

With his bronc still laden, he mounted and looked carefully around the ruined street. Darkness was rapidly sifting down over its sand-invaded straggle. There was only silence and the occasional whirl of dust and wavering of an ocotillo cactus stalk in the slight desert wind.

Clennan rode slowly down the ravaged course of the street, past the last of its ruins and headed for the open country. A hour and a half later, the yellowed lights of the windows of Rock Crossing came into view as the trail crested a hump of land.

Night shrouded the town's single street as he entered it. He found the place in no way changed since he was last there.

He rode slowly over the street's rutted surface. Light from windows of stores and saloons splashed over the boardwalks and on to the street and Clennan watched passing figures warily. No one seemed to recognize him. Night was now helping to obscure his identity but he wondered whether in the full light of day, he would be spotted by some resident who had known him in the old days. His chief worry concerned the Trillings' reward notice. Had it reached the law in this town? Had it been posted in a public place? Had the myth depicting Lew Clennan as a desperate badman spread this far? Might he be suddenly surprised by some reward-seeker or some brash youngster who fancied himself as a gunsharp?

Whatever the risks of venturing into Rock Crossing, they were less than those of a trip to Brimstone, since the reward poster had certainly reached Tinkettle Basin and it was essential that he sought supplies and ammunition. Furthermore, he and his bronc were weary. He had to take a chance on a spell of rest for both himself and the animal.

He found a livery stable and, with some satisfaction, noted that the lugubrious old man in charge was a stranger to him. He left the horse there to be fed, watered and bedded and, humping his war sack, crossed the street to the drab, false-fronted wooden structure of the hotel. In the dimly lit hall a young clerk half-dozed over a desk and came to life as Clennan approached him. He likewise, was a stranger and he gave a mechanical smile and a nod and reached for the register.

True to his earlier resolution, and as a stubborn point of honour Clennan signed his own name and, under 'Place of Residence' wrote 'Tinkettle Basin, AT'. No matter what misinformation the authorities in Purple Flats or the Trilling Detective Agency fed to the public, he was an innocent man in his own neck of the woods and he had no intention of hiding his identity.

Obviously, his name meant nothing to the young clerk who handed him a key tagged with the figure 5.

'Glad to have you with us, sir,' he said through his mechanical smile. 'Not many people in the hotel at present. You're sure to find things quiet and peaceable here.'

I hope so, thought Clennan.

'Good little restaurant right along the street if you're looking for supper, sir,' said the eager-to-please clerk. Clennan nodded his thanks, though he already knew the facilities offered by Rock Crossing.

Room 5 proved no better and no worse than the rooms he had known in many other frontier hotels and the bed looked reasonably comfortable. He dumped his war sack, then ventured out to the restaurant. He knew the place from earlier visits to Rock Crossing but found some alterations when he entered. In the old days it was kept by a brisk little German immigrant, but now a bustling and buxom woman appeared to be in charge. There were a few men in cowpoke gear eating at the tables, but none showed any interest in him. His luck was apparently holding. No one in Rock Crossing was yet rushing around yelling that Lew Clennan, the notorious, lead-throwing badman was in town.

The woman offered a welcome with some complaints about the infernal dryness of the spring weather, and served up a satisfying helping of sausage, potatoes, beans and gravy with ample apple-pie and coffee, the only decent food he had consumed since his overnight stay with Lars Lundgren.

Back at the hotel, he retired with the feeling that things were going better with this visit to Rock Crossing than he had expected. He was so totally unrecognized he almost forgot he was on the dodge.

The following morning brought an increased sense of anonymity. Refreshed by sleep, washed and shaved, he paid his hotel bill and ventured out to a still sleepy street. He breakfasted at the restaurant where the buxom woman was friendly but, like the other patrons in the place, paid him only scant attention.

He crossed the street to the livery stable, retrieved his bronc, saddled it and walked the animal out to the street where he had noted a grocery store with a gun shop close by. A wary glance cast in the direction of the town marshal's office and the jail showed only a languid young man wearing a deputy's star leaning against an upright support of the boardwalk awning and

smoking a cigarette. Clennan hoped the Trillings'
poster was not among those visible on the notice
board on the outer wall of the office.

The populace of Rock Crossing seemed not to
be interested in him in the slightest degree. The
Trillings' reward dodger might have penetrated
the community down in Tinkettle Basin, possibly
spreading alarm about him there but, up here on
the high tableland, he might just as well be invisi-
ble. He had not so far encountered any of the folk
he had known hereabouts in the days before he
departed from the MC ranch.

At the grocery store he spent a portion of his
carefully husbanded amount of money, filling his
war sack with canned meat and vegetables, a
couple of loaves of coarse bread and a supply of
coffee. In earlier times he had never much
frequented the stores of Rock Crossing and therefore never made any acquaintances among the
storekeepers. The half-asleep clerk who served
him did so with almost torpid boredom. Nor did
the owner of the gun store where he purchased
ammunition for his Colt revolver and his
Winchester show any greater curiosity about him.

Heartened by his continuing anonymity, he was
about to swing into his saddle outside the gun
store when a heavy hand fell on his shoulder and
gripped it hard.

Clennan whirled and his hand dived for his
holstered gun, then was stilled as he saw a broad,
tanned and youthful face grinning at him from
within the frame of a battered sombrero. It was a

familiar face, that of one of the crew from his father's bunkhouse in happier days on the MC ranch.

'Lew Clennan – after all these years!' said the young man. 'I saw you crossing the street and figured it was you. What're you doing in Rock Crossing?'

'Ted Orme!' breathed Clennan. 'It's good to see you, Ted. You're the first one of the old MC hands I've laid eyes on since I came back to this country.'

Ted Orme's grin faded. 'And, knowing you, Lew, I'd say you've returned for some purpose – what with just stepping out of a gun store, carrying a pack of ammunition and all.'

'Let's just say I have my plans,' replied Clennan darkly. 'But what're you doing these days? What about the rest of the MC wranglers?'

'I'm working for Dave Morgan's Running Steer outfit, a few miles back yonder. So are Shorty Harris and Buck O'Mara,' replied Orme. 'Old Dave took us on after we were all kicked off the MC by Brix and his gang. He's a good boss but things are not the same as in the old days on the MC with your old man, Frank, Ed and you. Young Jim Elks went back to Utah. He had a girl there and he was figuring on getting married anyway. Dad Steffans took the whole thing damned badly. Said he didn't want to work for any outfit but the MC and he was getting too blamed old for wrangling anyway. Said he was settling for a rocking-chair on the front porch of his widowed sister's house in California.'

'What about this business of being kicked off the

MC?' asked Clennan grimly. 'Did Brix replace the whole crew with his own men?'

'Yeah. Within days of Frank and Ed being buried. The whole crew of us hadn't recovered from the shock of it. We'd been trying to find some way of contacting you but nobody knew where you'd disappeared to. We were trying to keep the place running until maybe we did locate you and no one rightly knew what to do next when, one morning, Brix and a gang of his gun-toting ranni-hans rode on to the place. Brix said he had legal title to the whole outfit and we could pack up and ride. Didn't even pay us our time. Said there was no legal obligation to under the terms of his purchase.'

Lew Clennan snorted disgustedly. 'Terms of his purchase? Do you know anything about them, Ted?'

'Not much but the rumour was that he'd been trying to negotiate a sale through Horace Tait in your father's time and you know what happened to your father,' said Orme. 'Then, after you went, we heard that Brix was still attempting to buy the place and he wanted a meeting with Frank and Ed in Tait's office in Brimstone to make some kind of offer.'

'Say no more,' interposed Clennan. 'I know damn' well that Frank and Ed would never sell, but I suppose they went into Brimstone to say so and I'm sure they dealt out handfuls of hell to Brix and Tait.'

'Sure, and rode into a gun-trap in that grove of

trees on the way back,' said Ted Orme. 'And we know it was a gun-trap, though it was like your old man's death – done where there were no witnesses. It was a gun-trap, all right. Look, Lew, I know you well enough to guess you came back here on the prod, aching to smoke it out with Brix and his outfit. Give the word and I'll round up the rest of the MC boys. Every one of 'em will join up with you. I bet even old Dad Steffans will leave his rocking-chair and buckle on his gun.'

'No. I appreciate your loyalty, Ted, and I know the rest of the boys would throw in with me but it's not your fight. I'll tackle this my own way and I aim to settle things with Brix and his crew and with Horace Tait my own way. There's something else to be settled. The time owed to you and the others for the work you did. My old man and Frank and Ed never cheated the MC hands and I'm damned sure I never shall – and if I don't keep that promise it'll be because I've been killed trying!'

He swung into his saddle, bid a terse farewell to Ted Orme and rode for deserted Kimmins City.

Eli Brix stood on the gallery of the Slanted B ranch house, staring across the dusty expanse of the yard of his headquarters. Four hands were constructing a peeled-post corral in a distant corner, another pair were stacking cordwood against the wall of a plank outbuilding and a string of blue smoke was drifting across the scene from the tin smokestack of the cookhouse.

With screwed eyes, Brix looked beyond the activity immediately in front of him. He was a big, grim-faced man with a bulkiness which suggested power – and a love of power. He wore a beard, mostly black but streaked with grey and of that fullness which Civil War generals favoured. He sported a black broadcloth coat, which imparted a sort of respectability to a frame otherwise garbed in the costume of the cattle ranges. He had a Navy Colt holstered at his waist and his seamed face was shaded by a broad-brimmed black Stetson.

Next to him stood his foreman, Abe Crawley, a squat, ugly man of considerable physical strength who for years had shared his boss's dubious exploits. The eyes of both men were concentrating on a stirring of dust in the region of the arched gateway to the yard.

Shapes, blurred by distance and dust, were forming themselves into an approaching group of riders.

'Four of 'em,' commented Gawley to his boss. 'Looks like two are Dutton and Switzer.'

'Yeah, with a couple of guys in duster coats,' grunted Brix. 'Wonder who they are and what they want.' His nature was anything but hospitable and he did not like unexpected visitors turning up on his spread.

The owner of the Slanted B and his foreman watched as the four rode into the yard and headed for the house. Two were Dutton and Switzer, a pair of hard-bitten old hands who had migrated from the north with Brix's outfit. With them were a pair whose appearance matched that of any of the

Slanted B bunch when it came to rousing suspicions as to their integrity. One was lean and angular and the other shorter with a huge moustache.

'Bounty hunters,' muttered Brix. 'Got the brand all over 'em.'

The riders reined up in front of the gallery and Switzer called: 'Couple of gents who wandered on to our land, Mr Brix. We found 'em over on the west pasture. They say they'd like to have a few words with you.'

'Tell 'em to climb down,' Brix instructed. 'And it's *my* land – remember that!'

The pair in duster coats, both obviously trail-weary, descended from their saddles, walked the short distance to the gallery and mounted its steps.

'We're Reeder and Corkery, agents of the Trilling Detective Agency,' stated Clay Reeder.

'And you're looking for Lew Clennan,' supplied Eli Brix. 'Seth Wiseman, the marshal of Brimstone was over here the other day with a poster your people sent from Texas. You won't find Clennan on the Slanted B. If he shows up here, he'll likely meet hot lead.'

Brix paused, brushed a hand over his ample beard to hide a smirk and added piously: 'We don't like badmen at the Slanted B, and judging from the poster this Clennan has turned plumb bad. We can't take chances these days. There have been mysterious killings in this basin, y'know. There's too much deviltry around.'

Both Reeder and Corkery had mental reservations about this statement. The grapevine over a wide area of the West spoke of the spotty reputations of Eli Brix and those who rode with him but, as the man who was making himself the power in Tinkettle Basin, he might prove an ally in their search for Lew Clennan.

'Well, we'd appreciate any word of him if he does show up,' said Reeder.

'Oh, sure,' retorted Brix, abruptly shedding the amiability he showed at first. 'And you'd also appreciate the bonus of the reward offered by the Trillings alongside whatever they pay you as agents. Now, what were you doing on my land?'

The pair looked a little shamefaced and, again, Corkery left the talking to Reeder.

'Well, as a matter of fact, we sort of wandered on to it. We spent the night stranded on the edge of the salt flats back yonder. A damnfool old Dutchman who runs a horse ranch gave us directions to Brimstone and confused us. He was pretty confused himself, deaf as all hell and his English was lousy,' stated Clay Reeder.

'Is that so?' murmured Eli Brix, giving his beard a thoughtful stroke. 'Well, if you're still looking for Brimstone, it's northward, but I don't think you'll find Clennan there. Marshal Wiseman and his deputies are keeping their eyes peeled for him. If you've had a hard dry camp by the salt flats, you're welcome to the hospitality of the Slanted B. Blow your horses, give 'em water and feed and step over to the cookhouse for some grub.'

'Well, that's right neighbourly of you, Mr Brix,' said Slip Corkery, finding his voice for the first time.

'Think nothing of it,' responded Brix genially. 'Anyone in the basin will tell you we're friendly folk at the Slanted B. Tell the cook to fix you whatever you fancy.'

Reeder and Corkery dismounted and walked their weary horses towards the cookhouse. Both were feeling downright weary and used-up themselves. The dead-end trail on to which Lars Lundgren had directed them had led them into as uncomfortable a night as they had ever experienced, camping on the edge of trackless alkali flats on to which they dared not take their animals. This mission was proving a dreary, grinding and unavailing chore. It had not dawned on them that old Lars had deliberately misled them and they had reached the irksome conclusion that they had simply misunderstood his directions.

Eli Brix, standing beside his foreman on the gallery of the house, had reached his own conclusions concerning their meeting with the horse rancher.

'Did you hear what he said about some old Dutchman and a horse ranch?' he asked Abe Gawley.

'Sure. They were talking about old Lundgren, except he ain't a Dutchman and he ain't deaf. Seems like he was fooling those two.'

'Yeah, and he was a close friend of the Clennans. Remember how we heard that he took care of the funerals of the Clennan brothers when they had the misfortune to be bushwhacked?' answered Brix. 'My guess is that Lew Clennan is somewhere around this basin and old Lundgren knows it. He knew those jaspers were looking for him and he threw them off his trail. If Clennan's here, he aims to make trouble for us. We have to get to him before that dumb pair. I want to put him out of the way in my own style – and quick.'

'Maybe,' rumbled Gawley with heavy deliberation, 'we should pay that damned old Swede a call and find out what he knows.'

'That's exactly what I was thinking,' answered his boss, with another pensive stroke of his beard. 'I have an ache to settle Clennan's hash well before that pair yonder get a chance to collect any reward money. I just hope he's in the basin.'

Out in the yard, Reeder and Corkery approached the cookhouse. Two of the hands who had been set to creating the corral in the yard, a couple of younger hardcases who had recently been recruited by the Slanted B and who found they did not fully fit in with the old hands who had travelled to the south-west with Eli Brix, watched them pass with interest. Their loyalty to the Slanted B and its uncompromising owner was hardly cast-iron. It could easily be loosened if there was enough incentive – like the gathering of easy money.

'Got the look of bounty hunters,' commented Jesse Coote, a man of more solid bulk than his companion, Corey Blivens. 'They're on the trail, looking for someone.'

'Yeah, and you know the way my thoughts have been running after the marshal of Brimstone showed up with those reward dodgers,' replied Blivens.

Coote winced but he knew what Blivens meant. They had kept their mouths shut about a certain humiliating incident connected with a rider they encountered on the ridge trail and who had caused them to scrabble around the slippery shale of the ridge's slant in search of their weapons and saddles. The last things they wanted were a tongue-lashing from Eli Brix for being so easily duped when supposedly guarding the Slanted B's holdings and the ribald guffaws of the tough bunch in the bunkhouse. They had been hogtied and branded like a pair of tenderfeet up there on the ridge trail. It was not something they cared to think about or to have voiced abroad.

Marshal Seth Wiseman of Brimstone, who had become pretty much Eli Brix's man soon after the rancher began to show himself as the well-heeled embryo master of Tinkettle Basin, made it his business to ride out to the Slanted B headquarters with the Trillings' wanted posters. In fact, he showed far more diligence in warning Brix of the possibility of the last of the Clennans being in the region than in investigating the bushwhackings of Mark Clennan and his two sons. Jesse Coote and Corey Blivens, with other hands, had sight of those posters and, while the crude portrait they bore in no way resembled the man who had humiliated them, they wondered about him. Wondered and itched under a desire for revenge. And there was the tempting matter of that $500 reward.

The pair watched until Eli Brix had entered the house with the almost simian form of Abe Gawley trailing at his heels as usual. Then they left their corral-building chore and followed Reeder and Corkery into the cookhouse.

They found the pair talking to the ranch's cook, relaying Brix's orders to serve them and waited a while until the cook retreated and the two sat down at the big plank table. Coote plucked at Reeder's sleeve.

'You fellows looking for someone? Bounty hunters?' he asked.

Reeder looked up at him and bridled. He did not like that mercenary title. 'Detectives,' he stated indignantly. 'Detectives from the Trilling Agency in Texas. We're looking for someone – Lew Clennan. He killed a man in Texas, broke out of jail and tried to kill others, too. Why do you ask?'

'There's reward out. We've seen the posters,' said Coote. 'Is any of that reward to be shared? Does any of it go to folks giving information leading to his arrest?' He jerked his head towards Blivens and added: 'Him and me – we might know something.'

'Is that so?' said Reeder, looking highly interested. 'Sure, the reward will be shared out. There's a cut for anyone giving useful information. What do you know?'

'Well, we don't want Mr Brix or anyone here to know about it but we saw a guy on the ridge trail back yonder who might have been him. We never saw Clennan. We're not from these parts and only just took up with the Slanted B, but this fellow could have been him though he didn't look like the picture on the posters,' said Coote.

'They never do. Them artists who draw the pictures never see the wanted men either. They just do the same blamed face for all of 'em,' answered Reeder sourly. 'Where was he headed, this guy you saw?'

'Well, we just saw him in passing, you understand, but he was going up the trail.'

'What's up there?'

'Not that we know the country real well, but there's a big stretch of rangeland, some ranches and a town, Rock Crossing. Oh, and an old ghost town, so I hear.'

'So he might be up in that country and not down here in the basin?'

'Well, that's the way the *hombre* we met was headed, anyway,' confirmed Coote.

'If you nail him, don't forget it was us that pointed you to him,' put in Corey Blivens eagerly. 'It's Jesse Coote and Corey Blivens when it comes to paying a cut.'

'We'll remember you. I'll put your names in my book when we get back to our saddle-packs,' said Reeder.

The cook, visibly disconcerted at having to dance attendance on dusty strangers on Brix's orders, arrived and planted plates of hash, bread and a coffee-pot on the table. Coote and Blivens returned to their corral-building.

Slip Corkery forked a mouthful of grub into the

midst of his walrus moustache and growled: 'Where do you get off, promising that pair a cut of the reward? There's going to be no cut. We want what's on offer for ourselves – every cent of it!'

'Sure we do and that's the way it'll be,' Reeder smirked. 'Those two are just a couple of yokels. You can see they don't count worth a damn among the roughnecks of this outfit. But they had something to spill and it was worth hearing. As for promises, you've ridden with me long enough to know I'm the damndest liar.'

Corkery grinned. 'So are we going up the ridge trail to look for our man?' he asked.

'Yeah, but first we'll head for Brimstone to telegraph headquarters that we're hot on our man's track. It's essential that we keep their confidence in us topped up.'

Meanwhile, in the Slanted B ranch house, Eli Brix was fuming but keeping a grip on his temper. He had hoped that Lew Clennan had simply disappeared for good, but if he had indeed shown up in the Tinkettle Basin region, he could make trouble for Brix's huge ambitions just when everything was falling into his devious grasp. Where, however, *was* the prodigal of the Clennan family with the lead-throwing reputation?

It looked as if Lars Lundgren might have some answers. So Brix and Abe Gawley fell to making plans. Plans concerning Slanted B riders paying a night call on the old Swede.

CHAPTER FIVE

BULLETS IN BRIMSTONE

Lew Clennan rode back to the ghost town of Kimmins City bearing food and ammunition and mentally enumerating the priorities in his upcoming war.

First, he needed everyday finances, so he must obtain money from his long-standing account at the bank of Brimstone. Much had happened in his three years away from this country and, as Lars Lundgren had pointed out, Eli Brix as good as owned the town of Brimstone now. He hoped that this ownership did not extend to the bank and that its president was still old Jeff Samson, as honest a man as Brimstone ever held.

Secondly, he had to know about the deal by which the MC spread went into Brix's hands. It was clearly crooked and he had no doubt that the slippery lawyer Horace Tait could supply answers.

Thirdly, and the most crucial reason for his return to Tinkettle Basin, there was his gut-grinding yearning to discover the truth about the killings of his father and brothers and to wreak satisfaction for them. He needed no telling that the responsibility lay with the would-be emperor of Tinkettle Basin and his Slanted B outfit.

Once, his instincts would have urged him to plunge at Brix and his rannihans, slinging hot lead and the devil take the consequences, but his impetuosity of earlier years was now fined down to a more measured approach. He would achieve his aims step by step. He was fully aware, as Lars had reminded him, that he was taking on a big thing and he would tackle it with some forethought.

But he was sure that, in the end, hot lead would come into it in spades.

With the sun high, he reached Kimmins City and found it eerily still as usual without even the meagre desert breeze to stir the dust and weed in the nature-ravaged street. He dismounted, led his burdened horse over the rutted dust to the watering-hole to allow it to drink, then took down his purchases from behind his saddle and carried them to the old building which he had selected as his shelter. He stacked them in a dusty corner, returned to his bronc, took down his bedroll and carried it to the old store and laid it beside his cache of supplies.

His senses, heightened as was usual in the desert atmosphere, caused him to glance quickly through the dust-grimed glass of the window. He was sure he glimpsed a movement near the corner of a decayed adobe building across the street – a movement suggestive of someone just hastening around the corner and out of sight. Not some swift bird or jackrabbit but a human being.

Clennan remembered the previous day's curious sound of a carbine being pumped. His hand flew to his holster and came up as speedily, filled with his six-gun. He stepped quickly out on to the street.

Wary of a Winchester being loosed directly at him from that corner, he hastened across the street to the remains of the far boardwalk, all the time keeping his Colt levelled at the corner. He hugged the side of a warped plank building and crept towards the corner, reached it, halted for an instant then quickly stepped around the corner.

He found an 1875 pattern Winchester levelled squarely at him. It remained unshakably levelled even as the mouth of his own weapon remained just as firmly aimed at the slight figure holding the weapon – a figure clad in a dusty check shirt, worn jeans and a wide sombrero.

The two stood facing each other, frozen in confrontation, little more than a yard apart, each with a tightened trigger-finger and a hair-trigger temperament. Then Lew Clennan's mouth dropped open.

'Hell! You're a girl!' he exploded.

'I know it,' retorted the girl. 'I've known it all my life. I don't need you to tell me.'

'I damned near shot you,' said Clennan apologetically.

'You can still try if you think you can beat my speed but I warn you, I'll let daylight into your guts as soon as you twitch your finger,' said the girl, keeping her rifle firmly levelled at him.

Clennan lowered his gun, with his eyes fixed on the girl's face. It was heart-shaped, attractively freckled and tanned by open-air living. Wisps of blonde hair straggled down it from under her sombrero and her brows were slanted over bright-blue eyes. She was good and angry – and good and pretty into the bargain.

Clennan lowered his weapon but the girl still kept him covered. She made an aggressive figure and Clennan took in the Colt .45 which she wore at her waist, hitched to a well-filled shell-belt with a buckle of distinct Mexican design.

'You were hanging around here yesterday,' she said accusingly, 'and I nearly dropped you.'

'I heard you pump your rifle,' he responded.

'Sure, but you never saw me,' she said disdainfully. 'You looked around you like a startled jackrabbit. Like most men, you're plumb stupid. It never occurred to you to look up. That's where I was – not that you'd ever have seen me. I was lying on the roof of that old building a little along the street, hidden by the name-board at the front and watching you through a split in it. If I was sure you were one of Eli Brix's riders I would have killed you.' She paused, fixed him with a chilling glare and added icily: 'I'll still do it if you turn out

78

to be a Slanted B man.'

There was no mistaking her determination but Clennan met it with a wry smile. 'Ma'am, I've done some shameful things in my time, but riding for Eli Brix is not one of them, nor ever likely to be. You can wager on it,' he said.

This caused the girl's expression to soften slightly but she still kept the Winchester levelled at him. He now knew that, in the matter of Brix and his outfit, he and the girl were on the same side so he took a chance and holstered his six-gun. The Winchester, however, remained pointed at him.

'I'd like to be sure of it but I'm not interested in soft talk from you, mister and I'm not listening to any explanations. You've been fixing like you aim to stay here, toting your bedroll and gear into that old store yonder. I'd prefer to see you ride to hell and gone,' she stated.

'But I *do* intend to stay,' he said firmly. 'I guess you have no more right to claim Kimmins City than I have. You can't kick me out.'

Through his head raced questions concerning this girl. Who was she? Why was she so well-armed? Why was she here? He remembered the sign around the well: the plain evidence of a horse and a mule. Mules were used to carry burdens. Someone had been hauling something into this forlorn place on a pack-mule and the conclusion that this girl was involved in that activity was inescapable.

She had made it clear that she was no friend of Eli Brix and the Slanted B and this placed them on common ground. He wanted to know more, to make a truce with her but the Winchester remained only too obviously ready to be discharged at him despite his peaceful gesture of holstering his weapon. She might be an enemy of Brix but she clearly had no desire to discuss the matter with Clennan. The mouth of her carbine remained menacing and her eyes still blazed hostility.

Then, for a space, her gaze softened and she asked: 'Are you alone?'

'Yes'.

'Do you swear it?'

'Yes. I swear it.'

'You're right,' she said slowly. 'I can't get rid of you short of shooting you. You say you're not connected with Brix and maybe you're not. Then again, you might be a liar. I'll tell you nothing about what I'm doing here except that I'm camped just a little way back yonder on the edge of town. I'm warning you that, if you stay here for whatever purpose, I want no smart-alecky man-trouble from you – you know what I mean.'

'Sure, I know what you mean, lady, but I have things to do and dalliances are not on my schedule,' he said.

Her mouth tightened as if she was not wholly convinced but wavering.

'I want access to that water yonder at all times with no interference from you. I don't give a damn who you are or what you've done so long as you keep to yourself and keep well away from me,' she stipulated with her gaze fixed on his face. 'Stay on that far side of the street and it'll be a case of I've not seen you and you've not seen me if anyone asks.'

It looked like the dawning of a truce and, possibly, she was encouraged towards it by his gesture of holstering his Colt, but her blue eyes remained steely and still suspicious.

The girl began to walk backwards along the weed-choked straggle of alleyway at the mouth of which they stood, with the Winchester still pointing at his midriff. Almost at the end of the alley, she called: 'One last thing. I'm not alone here – remember that!'

Then she slipped quickly out of sight around the back of the plank building. A brief space afterwards there came the sound of receding hoofs.

'Well, if that don't beat all,' Clennan breathed. 'A girl holed up in a place like this. And someone's obviously been hauling something up here by mule. It can only be her or whoever's with her – unless she's bluffing and is really alone.'

He strode back across the street, puzzled by the interlude with the young woman. She was certainly a good-looking girl but no blushing violet. She knew what she was doing when she handled a carbine and she looked as if she would not hesitate to use it if provoked.

'Whoever she is and whatever her game is, she's cut from the old rock when it comes to guts,' he told himself.

He reached his bronc, left on the sparse graze

surrounding the water-source. He ensured that the animal had another sparing drink in readiness for more travel and checked over the ammunition in the chambers of his Colt and in the loops of his shell-belt. He took his rifle from its saddle-scabbard, walked back to the supplies he had stashed in the old store, replenished its magazine from his newly purchased batch and shoved an amount of spare ammunition for both six-gun and rifle into the pockets of his shirt and pants.

For the first time since his return to Arizona Territory, the prodigal with a six-gun was going into Brimstone – the town where his enemy, Eli Brix, now held sway.

Clennan rode to the end of the street and reached the rim, which gave a panoramic view of the basin below. He could see the ridge trail from that point and it bore no sign of any traffic. He nevertheless decided to take one of the lesser, little-travelled scrub-shrouded trails which slithered down the escarpment of land frowning over the basin.

He searched his memory, to recall the location of these age-old Indian hunters' tracks he had known well in his boyhood. He found one and took the bronc cautiously down it. It was ill-defined, cluttered with catclaw and Spanish dagger and rearing saguaro cactus. Sometimes man and horse were dwarfed by an abundance of desert scrub.

And, all the time, the enigma of the rifle-toting girl in Kimmins City was on his mind.

The vague trail led down to the floor of Tinkettle Basin where Clennan picked up a more defined track, a backtrail into town. With the heat now more intense, he saw Brimstone's scatter of buildings coming into view over a rise in the terrain. He wondered just how strong the writ of Eli Brix ran there and reflected that he might find out soon enough.

He rode cautiously into the town's single street and found things in no way changed. Brimstone was no bigger and certainly no lovelier than before. It was still just a border country cowtown, a collection of plank and adobe buildings, sweltering in torpid heat.

There were a few people on the plankwalks and he wondered how many might have seen the Trillings' reward dodger and recognize him. He yanked his hat-brim well down over his face as a precaution.

He was taking chances by being here and one of them was on whether the Brimstone bank was still controlled by Jeff Samson. In the days before the arrival of Eli Brix, Samson was a pillar of the community and he knew the Clennan family well. Disturbingly, however, there was a chance that Samson was now dead for he had not been young when Lew Clennan was a kid.

Clennan planned a visit to the bank – but not if it had gone into the grasp of Brix.

He saw the bank, a solid brick structure, one of the most substantial in Brimstone and was heartened to see, still emblazoned on its signboard:

JEFFERSON SAMSON, PRESIDENT.

Almost exactly across the street was the office of the town marshal, Seth Wiseman. It was a low adobe building and the door was open but there was no sign of life in its vicinity. A little distance along that same side of the street was the concern which was Clennan's immediate objective, a building whose discreetly blacked-out windows bore peeling gold-leaf letters reading: HORACE TAIT, ATTORNEY-AT-LAW.

The hitch rack outside the office was empty and Clennan angled his horse at a walk over the street towards it. He dismounted, hitched his rein to the rack, strode to the door of the office, opened it and walked in. The outer office was empty save for a bald and otherwise nondescript little man sitting at a small desk. This was Walter Gross, Tait's clerk, who jumped visibly when he saw the newcomer.

'Lew Clennan!' he gasped and his expression made it plain that he had seen the wanted posters. Behind him was the door of an inner office to which Clennan nodded.

'Is Mr Tait in?' he asked.

'Yes,' replied Gross with a scared gulp.

'Good.' Clennan patted the butt of his holstered Colt meaningfully, causing Gross to quake. 'Now, stand up and lock that front door, Mr Gross.'

Gross moved quickly, complying with the order, all the time watching Clennan out of the corner of his eye. After the street door was locked, Clennan drew his Colt and waved it towards the inner door.

'Open the door and let's go see Mr Tait. You go

in first,' he said with a hard edge to his voice. Gross did so and entered Tait's office on quaking legs with Clennan following him with a naked gun.

Horace Tait was sitting at a desk and behind him was a tall iron safe. He was a thin, stoop-shouldered man, sharp-nosed and with sparse, sandy hair. He looked up in alarm when his scared clerk entered with Clennan following, flourishing his revolver. Clennan kicked the door closed behind him and gave the lawyer an unfriendly grin.

'Clennan!' Tait gurgled. 'You're a wanted man. Where the hell have you come from?'

'Never mind where I came from – I'm here. And I'm here to talk serious business,' stated Clennan.

Tait's pale eyes were wide open and he was now sitting bolt upright with fear. 'What do you want here?' he mouthed.

'To talk about the deal passing the MC outfit into Eli Brix's hands,' Clennan said icily. 'There's supposed to have been an agreement drawn up between my brothers and Brix. I want to know about it.'

'It was legal – all legal,' blustered the lawyer. 'It was all properly drawn up and signed by your brothers.'

Lew Clennan gave a twisted grin but there was no humour in his eyes, fixed unwaveringly on Tait's white face.

'It was not legal,' said Clennan. 'My brothers would never do a deal with Brix. They would never sign anything away to Brix and I had a legal stake in the MC. Any proper agreement would need my signature. This whole thing was faked. Into the bargain, after my brothers came into town to talk over some phony deal, Brix had them bush-whacked just as my father was bushwhacked. Now give me the story – the truth.' He emphasized his impatience by raising the Colt and holding its mouth an inch away from the end of Tait's nose. 'I want answers, Tait. You've seen the posters, I take it – the allegations of murder and attempted murder in Texas. Don't dally with me. I'm in no mood for gentle treatment.'

In the background, he could almost hear the teeth of Walter Gross chattering and the clerk found his voice, jittering huskily: 'Mr Clennan. I didn't have anything to do with any of it. I only work here.'

'And something did go on right here in this office, didn't it, Mr Gross?' growled Clennan with-out taking his eyes off the scared Tait. 'There was trickery, faked documents and faked signatures, and Mr Tait here is going to talk about it or I'll blow his head off.' Now he touched the end of the lawyer's nose with the muzzle of his pistol.

'All right, all right,' gasped Horace Tait, fighting for breath. 'I fixed it all for Brix.'

'Fixed it by criminal means and you were proba-bly a party to the killing of my brothers,' said Clennan. 'In fact the whole so-called legal land deal was probably faked after their deaths. Oh, sure, there was some kind of preliminary meeting set up to bring Frank and Ed into town to give the appearance of a deal being negotiated, but that

86

SIX-GUN PRODIGAL

was only a blind. Their deaths were already arranged. Maybe you helped plot my father's death earlier, too. You had a plenty big hand in helping Brix get his paws on the MC.'

'No,' denied the quaking Tait. 'No, I had nothing to do with any killings. I swear it. I had no part in any of that.'

'The papers concerning the deal. Where are they?' demanded Clennan.

'In my safe.'

'Get them.'

Tait stood quickly, fumbled in a pocket and produced a set of keys. He turned to the safe behind his chair and unlocked it with shaking hands. From the interior he produced a set of documents, tied with legal ribbon. Lew Clennan took them, still holding the lawyer under the menacing mouth of his Colt. He glanced quickly at the clerkly legend written across the front cover: *Agreement of land sale between Eli Brix and Frank and Edward Clennan.*

'It's crooked as hell,' scorned Clennan. 'Any agreement would require my involvement and my signature.'

'I didn't have anything to do with forgery, Mr Clennan,' wailed Tait's clerk. 'I only wrote out the terms. I didn't write any signatures.'

'I guess Mr Tait can tell us the whole truth about the signatures,' responded Clennan, grinning. 'See here, Tait. Tinkettle Basin might be at the back of beyond. We haven't even got a properly organized county or county sheriff and the law in

87

Brimstone isn't worth calling law. But there's a US marshal in Tucson and these documents will be passed on to him.'

The lawyer was shivering all over, opening and shutting his mouth, trying to find words. At length he croaked: 'You'll – you'll ruin me, Clennan.'

'Damn right I will and it'll be a pleasure.' Clennan's grin was as attractive as that of a wolf. 'If I were in your shoes, I'd pack my sack right now and run for Mexico. Try following me with a firearm when I leave and I'll drop you pretty damn quick.' He backed towards the door of the office, keeping the gun levelled at Tait while Gross had flattened himself against the wall. He let himself out of the room, walked through the outer office and unlocked the street door.

He walked his bronc the short distance over the street to the bank, tethered the animal there and entered. A couple of tellers, one vaguely familiar, watched him from behind the counter. The place was empty of customers and a glance towards the glass-windowed inner office of Jeff Samson revealed the banker there, more white-haired now and leaning over a desk. Samson looked up, saw Clennan and came out of the office with an extended hand.

'Why, Lew – after all this time!' he exclaimed. Then the suggestion of heartiness changed and his face became clouded. 'I can't tell you how sorry I was about your father and brothers.'

'Sure, Mr Samson. It was all ugly and it might be you've heard some ugly tales about me,' Clennan said. 'Do I have to tell you it's all lies?'

'You don't, Lew. I've heard reports and seen the posters outside the marshal's office but I knew you and your family too well to believe anything but the best of you. And it's still that way. But you're on dangerous ground here in Brimstone, particularly with those posters in circulation. You know what's been going on in this basin and things are not getting any better. Watch your step. Now, what can we do for you?'

'I've had an account here for years and I want to withdraw about three hundred for immediate expenses,' said Clennan. 'One thing first, though. I take it Eli Brix has no stake in this bank?'

Jeff Samson gave an ironic laugh. 'He sure hasn't. He has a finger in nearly every pie in Brimstone and total control of a good many but there's one concern he'll never get into while I'm breathing and that's the Brimstone bank.'

'Good,' said Clennan. 'Do you have a large legal-sized envelope?'

'I'll see you get one.' The banker beckoned to the teller who looked familiar to Clennan. 'Henry, you remember Mr Clennan. He's an old customer. Be good enough to bring him a withdrawal blank and a large envelope. And, Henry, don't say anything about seeing him around here.'

The teller nodded, complied with Samson's instructions and Clennan filled out the blank form, drawing on his long-established account. He then drew the documents from Tait's safe from inside his shirt, put them into the envelope and wrote on it: *Lewis Clennan. Private. To be opened only by Lewis Clennan or in the event of his death only by United States Marshal, Tucson, Arizona Territory.*

Clennan sealed the envelope and handed it to Jeff Samson.

'Mr Samson, I understand the bank undertakes to hold valuable property for its customers. Will you please keep this in your safe until I call for it or until events give you cause to hand it to the named authority?' he said gravely.

The banker took the envelope, read the words and raised his eyebrows. 'I will, Lew,' he said. And, with a banker's professional integrity, made no further mention of the matter but commented: 'You're deep into something, I know, Lew and I wish you well – so will a great many in the basin – but, as I told you, watch your step. Brimstone can be mighty dangerous for you.'

Clennan walked out of the bank with $300 of much needed money in his billfold and the satisfaction of having taken a decisive action against Eli Brix which could have the added bonus of ruining a lawyer who was anything but an ornament to his profession.

The euphoria died almost immediately.

He had not even reached his tethered horse when, from the direction of Horace Tait's office across the street, there came an alarmed and anguished screech. He saw that the lawyer had somehow overcome his paralysis of fear and had staggered out of his office. Wild-eyed and waving his arms, he was yelling: 'Marshal Wiseman! I've

been robbed! I've been robbed by Lew Clennan!'
He ceased his bawling for a instant as he caught
sight of Clennan leaving the bank. Then he
resumed on higher note of panic: '*Look! There he is!
Now he's robbed the bank!*'

A woman further along the plankwalk from
Clennan screamed and ran for cover and a man
somewhere roared: 'Lew Clennan! Hell, he's
wanted for murder, ain't he?'

Horace Tait, obviously fearful that Clennan
might start shooting at him from across the street,
had scooted back into his office.

A split second earlier, two stringy riders in
duster coats had arrived in the street, just at the
moment when the lawyer's accusation of bank
robbery was being screeched through the air.

'Clennan!' spat Clay Reeder. 'Hell, it's him –
and he's just robbed the bank!' He spurred his
horse forward, unshipping his revolver at the same
time. Beside him, Slip Corkery did likewise.
Reeder loosed a wild shot as his mount jogged
onward. Clennan, almost at the hitch rack, heard
the bark of the weapon and dropped to the scuffed
planks of the walk, drawing his Colt as he hit the
surface. The few townsfolk who had been in the
vicinity of the bank were hastening away in panic
and Reeder and Corkery were charging up the
street, flourishing their sixguns.

Belly down on the planks, Clennan managed to
get off a shot in their general direction and the
bullet whanged close enough to Corkery's head to
bite a chunk out of his hat and make the Trilling

agents realize that, seated high in their saddles, they were vulnerable targets.

Snarling and spitting in anger, they quickly pulled leather, dismounted in the middle of the street and lay down with their guns aimed at Clennan, sprawling on the plankwalk near the bank.

Clennan rolled over rapidly as they blasted shots in his direction and the bullets hammered chips out of the edge of the walk only inches from his head. He was aware of his tethered horse, prancing and jerking in alarm as the gunfire exploded around it. On the far side of the street, behind the Trilling operatives, he could see Seth Wiseman, the town marshal, and a deputy come cautiously and bewilderedly out of their office with drawn six-guns. For an instant they appeared to be hypnotized by the vivid drama unfolding before their eyes, then they immediately dropped to the plankwalk.

Lew Clennan rolled further along the scarred planks and was now closer to his bronc, coming to rest outside a dry-goods store which had barrels and packing-cases stacked before it. He rolled beside a barrel, rose to a squat and triggered another couple of defensive slugs at Reeder and Corkery who at once began to emulate Clennan's tactic, rolling over in the rutted and fouled street to avoid Clennan's shots.

Clennan calculated his chances of reaching his bronc, which was in danger of being hit as the gunfire barked and sent echoes clattering through the air. From what he could see of the marshal and deputy on the far side of the street, they were still bewildered, trying to discover what the shooting was about.

He was aware that, at any moment, the pair of lawmen might join in the fray and the odds against him would then be doubled. At that very moment a gun blasted and he felt a harsh, stinging sensation in his upper left arm as hot lead tore through his shirtsleeve and nicked the flesh. Gasping, he rolled further into the shelter of the barrel, then decided on taking a chance.

He rose and loped the several paces towards his horse.

He knew he must reach the animal before the pair in the middle of the street and before the marshal and his deputy began to join in the attack.

Requiring both hands to unhitch the reins from the rack, he holstered his Colt, grabbed the leathers, gritted his teeth against the sting of his flesh wound and fought to calm the jittery bronc. Then he forked the saddle. With the tail of his eye he saw the men in duster coats rising from their lying positions and calming their own panicking horses while also taking their Henry rifles from their saddle scabbards.

Just as he spurred the bronc forward, he heard Marshal Seth Wiseman bellowing from the far plankwalk: 'What the hell's happening?' As the animal plunged forward, one of the pair in the middle of the street yelled back: '*It's Clennan. He's robbed the bank*!'

Clennan sprawled his upper body along the

neck of his mount as it bounded forward, glad to be escaping from the close proximity of blasting gunfire. The harsh roar of a Henry slammed across the street. Clennan ducked his head yet lower and a bullet screamed high over it.

Controlling the horse with one hand, he unholstered his six-gun again and pegged a shot back at the hostile group on the street, then swerved the animal to bolt into an alleyway.

He was now in almost the same position as when he hared it out of Purple Flats. Though he now had a wounded arm which he suspected was bleeding, he at least had the advantage of being familiar with the environs of Brimstone. He knew that beyond the buildings of the town lay the region into which he was now heading – that tangled scrubland which he had traversed when coming into town. He made for it, urging every spark of energy out of his mount.

He was speedily clear of town and all was clear behind him, but he knew it would not remain so for long. The scrubland baked in a heat haze ahead of him and he made for it, urging all the speed the bronc was capable of. The flesh wound in his arm stung and he reflected that, knowing he was taking chances in entering Brimstone, he had scored a success against Tait, but now affairs had gone grotesquely awry.

Back in town, Marshal Seth Wiseman was still trying to figure out the meaning of the events on the street, though he had recognized Clennan and knew that he was indeed the returned prodigal of

Tinkettle Basin, who bore no resemblance to the portrait on the reward dodger at that moment nailed outside his office. The lawman had at first thought the two strangers involved in the shooting were outlaws and that a gang was in process of robbing the bank, but it now dawned on him that they must be agents of the Trilling Agency who, according to advance intelligence, were on Clennan's trail.

Wiseman belatedly saw that action was called for. There was bad blood between Eli Brix and the Clennans, three of whom were now dead. He had not enquired with any great diligence into the deaths of the senior Clennan and his sons. The killings were, so far as he was concerned, the work of persons unknown, criminal random attacks. For, since his arrival, Eli Brix had worked a potent magic in certain sections of local society through his deep purse and strong-arm crew. Palms had been greased, among them that of Marshal Seth Wiseman, who was hardly an exemplary law officer. Wiseman found it profitable to be friendly to the Slanted B and its owner. One knew on which side one's bread was buttered that way.

Now he began to reason that the return of Lew Clennan with his gun reputation could only mean trouble for Brix and the Slanted B. Seth Wiseman knew he must do something about it if he was to keep his bread buttered on the right side.

Hank Venner, Wiseman's deputy, showing more initiative that the marshal, was already running for the alleyway which led to the stable housing the lawmen's horses. In the middle of the street Clay Reeder was mounting his horse, while Slip Corkery was trying to calm his jittery animal with one hand and ruefully examining the bullet hole in his hat, held in the other.

Eventually mounted, the Trilling agents charged forth towards the alley down which Clennan had disappeared.

Out at the back of town, Clennan's mount was pounding the dry earth, flat out for the scrub. A quick glance over his shoulder showed him that there was not yet any pursuit but he knew it would come. His hope was to get into that expanse of scrubland where the growth was higher than a mounted man and lose himself and the bronc from view before pursuers had sight of him.

He reached the scrub, throwing another backward glance for a fleeting glimpse of the back of Brimstone's main street and the alleys which opened into the wide land at the rear of the town. Then he and his mount were deep in the harsh vegetation and he lost all sight of the town. Mentally, he juggled with choices of strategy. Should he swing north and head for the dim trails leading up to the tableland above the basin and his hiding-place in Kimmins City, or make a break for the rangelands here in the basin? Whichever he chose, he knew he would be the object of intense and savage interest to Eli Brix once he got word of the doings in Brimstone.

For the present there was a distinct danger of pursuit from the town, indeed, the two Trilling agents came thundering out of the alleyway at the instant Clennan bolted into the brush.

Marshal Seth Wiseman had lost some time bawling for a posse of citizenry to no effect, but when he and Venner were in their saddles they went galloping in the wake of dust left by the two agency men.

Emerging into the open from the alley, the pursuers saw no sign of man or bronc and, in scrub towering higher than his hat, Lew Clennan knew that, unseen though he might be, his flight would stir up banners of dust from the parched land to betray his whereabouts.

So he decided on a bold and calculated strategy.

CHAPTER SIX

ACTION ON THE HOME RANGE

Eli Brix strutted around the ranch yard of the Slanted B, glowering at a gathering of his hands. They had presented themselves in response to an urgent order from the rancher and there was a mood of almost gleeful anticipation among them. Mostly, they were as unsavoury a bunch as could be found along a long stretch of the border, the bulk of them being trigger-tripping veterans of Brix's participation in the cattle wars up north; the likes of his foreman, Abe Gawley and ruffians such as Dutton and Switzer.

The two younger drifters who had recently signed on, Blivens and Coote, were hanging back at the rear. They knew this conclave had to do with Lew Clennan's presence somewhere in this country. They were pretty sure the man they had encountered on the ridge trail was Clennan but they kept their mouths tightly shut. They had no desire for Eli Brix to know how he had humiliated them or how he had slipped through their fingers when they were supposed to be watching the fringes of the Slanted B ranges. Nor did they want Brix to know what had passed between themselves and the two Trilling agents concerning a portion of the reward. Better to keep tight as clams and swim with the rest of the crew.

And the crew was fixing to make big trouble.

'That damned old Swede knows something about Clennan,' bellowed Brix. 'He was a friend of the Clennans and he sure enough put those two Trilling men on a wrong trail because he knew where Clennan went. My guess is Clennan called on him and he knows where Clennan is now.' The rancher paused and savoured a new thought, then exploded: 'Hell, he might even be holed up at Lundgren's place right now for all we know!'

'So you want Clennan found, Mr Brix?' queried one of his veteran riders, nudging his holstered six-gun.

'Damn right I do,' growled Brix. 'I want a bunch of you to pay a call on old Lundgren and find out what he knows about Clennan. He's usually on his own up at that horse outfit yonder, so you'll have no trouble handling him. If he doesn't co-operate, deal with him the way you dealt with Harry Siggs. If Clennan is loose in Tinkettle Basin, he means trouble and I don't aim to have him louse up my operations. Remember, I brought some vitality to

99

this half-asleep basin and so long as money rolls in from cattle and silver, you jaspers will make the easiest livings you'll ever make. Round up the rest of the hands, saddle up and ride out as soon as dusk falls.' He paused, looked at the knot of men and singled out Corey Blivens, one of the pair of newest recruits and jabbed a finger towards him. 'Hey, you. Ed Snead and Lafe Barnard are stationed up at the northern line camp on the old Clennan pastures. Ride out there and bring them in. I want them in on this move. Get on your cayuse!'

Blivens swallowed hard. Since he and Coote had taken up with the Slanted B he had many times realized that they were out of their depth among the outfit's crew, gunsharps hardened by years of dubious dealings on the northern rangelands under Brix's command. Ed Snead and Lafe Barnard, currently guarding the graze acquired just as dubiously from the Clennans' MC outfit at one of the far-flung line camps, were two of the longest serving and most uncouth of the bunch.

'Tell 'em to come ready for a little shooting sport,' stipulated Brix as Blivens moved towards his corralled horse.

And the would-be ruler of all Tinkettle Basin chuckled within his ample beard. 'Yeah. That's what it'll be,' he muttered. 'Shooting sport! And I'll sure settle Lew Clennan's hash at the end of it!'

At the very moment when the two Trilling riders and the lawmen emerged from the alleyway into the wide land backing the town, Lew Clennan, deep in the high scrub, pulled the bronc to a halt and swung out of the saddle. He yanked hard on the leathers to bring the animal down to its knees. Sprawling beside the horse, he soothed it, hoping it would not whinny, hauled his Winchester from its saddle scabbard and thumbed fresh ammunition into the chambers of his Colt. He was fairly sure nothing of himself or the animal could be seen above the growths and that his disappearance into the scrubland had not been noted by the pursuers, whom he now knew to be on the scene because he could hear the drumming of horses and hoarse, bewildered yells.

'Which way did he go?' bawled one, somewhere on the fringe of the scrub.

'He beat it across the scrub! Got plumb out of sight!' answered another.

'He couldn't have,' shrilled a thin, reedy voice, recognizable as that of Marshal Seth Wiseman. 'He didn't have time.'

Clennan, biting his lip against the gnawing sting of the wound in his arm, holstered his Colt and came to his knees but kept his head well below the top of the scrub. He hefted the Winchester one-handedly. He would play the Indian game and lie low. If the searchers plunged into the thick of the scrub and came on him, he would gamble on a surprise tactic, suddenly standing up and firing point blank. From what he had seen on the street, there were four of them: Wiseman, Venner and the pair who were surely Trilling operatives. Swift and decisive action would be called for against such odds because, believing he had robbed the bank, they were sure to begin shooting mercilessly on sight.

He would have to follow his initial shot with three immediate and fatal ones to take care of the remaining hunters.

At once, such an action would properly make him an outlaw where, so far, he bore that stigma undeservedly. He was being forced into the position of killing or being killed.

He crouched low, scarcely daring to breathe and realizing that all his plans could unravel through a move made by any of the four searching riders whom he heard floundering around somewhere near the edges of the scrubland. Although unseen, they were near enough for him to catch their snarling and cursing and feel the ground vibrating under the thump of their horses. Perspiration trickled from under his hat-brim; his finger tightened on the trigger of the rifle and the gunshot wound in his arm nagged.

The sound of the riders' activities rose and fell, then tension climbed within him as he heard the tramp of a horse and a stirring of brush not too far away. He gripped the carbine, ready to spring up out of the vegetation like an Apache on a desert raid and get in the first shot before the mounted man had an opportunity to shoot on locating him.

Then abruptly, the sound stopped and the unseen rider yelled on a disgruntled note: 'Hell, we could search this country all day. He's clean

102

hightailed it, I tell you. We can't even see his dust.' Clennan suspected it was the voice of the deputy, Venner.

There was a diminishing hoof-tramp and the stirring of vegetation lessened, suggesting that the rider was moving away.

'Blast it! We *would* search all this country if Corkery and me weren't on horses that're all tuckered out with travelling,' responded another voice, equally disgruntled. That, reasoned Clennan, must be one of the Trilling pair. 'But, by thunder, we know he's in this basin and we'll get him,' continued the voice. 'Anyway, we have to get to the telegraph office and contact headquarters.'

Doubtless to tell the Trilling bosses that you're only inches away from catching Lew Clennan and to keep that reward warm for you, mused Clennan. *Well, we'll see about that!*

The sounds of searching horsemen receded, then ceased completely, and Clennan guessed they had returned to the town. Still, he lay low, soothing the kneeling bronc, keeping his head low and waiting. And waiting.

There had been a witness to the gun-noisy drama on the street of Brimstone, unseen by its participants and, indeed, wholly unnoticed by the citizens who scattered in alarm as weapons barked and lead flew. Furthermore, he had remained unnoticed by Lew Clennan during the whole of Clennan's ride from Kimmins City to the town but, riding a dun pony, he had been close on Clennan's tail, tracking him with a tenacity and a rare skill which enabled him to make himself and his mount almost part of the landscape.

His name was Nacio – just Nacio. He was a Mexican, part of Spanish line and a greater part of Yaqui Indian line. Nacio had been raised by the Yaqui and schooled in their stoic skills of desert endurance. He could track a man from a given point to the last inch of the known world without ever revealing himself until he was ready.

It was a measure of Nacio's skill that, throughout Clennan's journey, he had shadowed him along the vague trails and through the scrub country without Clennan's having any inkling that a slight figure in a serape and a sombrero as anonymously dun-coloured as his mount was close on his heels. As Clennan entered the main street of Brimstone, Nacio peeled away and established himself and his animal behind the crumbled remains of an adobe wall, a relic of the first days of the settlement. There, unseen by the townsfolk and Clennan, he watched.

With impassive Indian eyes, he saw Clennan visit Tait's office, then progress to the bank. He witnessed the lawyer's belated emergence from his premises, his hysterical accusations of robbery and the subsequent gunplay on the panicking street. As Clennan made his getaway with the lawmen and the two strangers in pursuit, Nacio slipped away from his post at the tail-end of the street. He was just in time to see, from the corner of a building at the back of town, Clennan disappear into the high brush and he watched the searchers scout the margins of the brush, then give up and ride back to Brimstone.

He gave a satisfied grunt, spurred his pony and set off north, returning up to the tableland and Kimmins City by way of those same dim and half-forgotten trails.

On the further side of the ghost-town from where Clennan had established his headquarters, he came to a rock-face behind the abandoned ruins. It was riddled with excavations, some small and some gaping cave-mouths. For Kimmins City had suffered the fate of many such hard-luck mining-camps. After the failure of the initial strike, a horde of hopefuls had descended on the place, refusing to believe that the meagre streak Old Man Kimmins had found was exhausted. They dug frenziedly in random spots, even hollowing out pigeon-holes and caves in the rock-face to discover what Old Man Kimmins could have told them they would find – nothing!

Nacio dismounted close to a large, cavelike excavation in the rock-face. The dry earth around the opening showed evidence of trampling by human and animal traffic and a slim young man in serape and sombrero sat on a rock, cleaning a carbine. He gave the newcomer a perfunctory nod as he entered the cave.

In the gloomy excavation there were several stout boxes stacked against a wall that bore the marks of the hopeless hewings of the desperate ore-seekers who had created this extensive hole in the rock. Each was marked by an exclamation mark in red paint. It meant danger, even to those unable to read.

The gloom at the back of the cave disgorged a slender figure in boyish garb: the girl who had earlier held Lew Clennan at rifle point.

'Well?' she asked. 'What's his game?'

'Robbery,' said Nacio. 'He robbed the Brimstone bank and got clean away.' His English was clipped, precise and Americanized, suggesting an educated background.

'Robbery!' The girl gave a low whistle. 'So he *is* Clennan, the one the Trillings have put out posters for and whose family owned the MC outfit?'

'No doubt of it. He doesn't look like the drawing on the dodger but Tait, the lawyer, was yelling his name all over the street. He went into Wiseman's office first, and seems to have stolen something from him. Tait came charging out, bawling that Clennan had robbed him.'

The girl's attractive eyes crinkled in amusement. The thought of a blow struck against the lawyer obviously pleased her. 'Tait is Brix's man and the Clennans were victims of Brix, or so the story goes,' she commented. 'Whatever Clennan's reasons for setting up camp here on our roost are, I guess he was truthful about not being connected with Brix and he surely wasn't spying for Brix. He might go in for bank robbery on the side but I'd say we're allied in the same cause.'

'No, he wasn't spying on us and he certainly has no idea of what we're planning,' affirmed Nacio.

'He went to ground in the scrubland behind the town. I could have tracked him down but figured I'd seen all I needed.' He nodded to the stacked boxes with their vivid warning markings and asked: 'We cut loose tonight?'

The girl drew her mouth into a tight, determined line. 'Sure. Tonight, just as we planned,' she stated.

Crouched in the high scrub, Lew Clennan listened. The last sounds of departing horses had died away. His wound stung and he was aware that the sleeve of his shirt was sodden with blood and his mouth was dry. His kneeling bronc was shifting with restlessness and discomfort. Clennan reached up with one hand, found his big desert canteen at the saddle horn, uncorked it one-handedly and took a meagre drink. Enduring some discomfort in his injured arm, he managed to pour water into his cupped hand and moisten the animal's lips. He wondered at what rate he was losing blood but was aware that the bone of his arm was uninjured.

'Damn it!' he growled to the bronc. 'I need some kind of dressing on this arm.'

Suddenly, he was aware of his proximity to the northern pastures of what had been the MC outfit. He could reach the outlying fringes of his family's old holdings by a short, looping ride through the scrub country and along a dried watercourse which would place him on the outer fringes of the MC's graze. He remembered that located there was a line-cabin. In his father and brothers' day it was empty through the summer months, being occupied by a line rider only through the winter to ensure the safety of the stock. Even this far south, in the higher country, there were heavy rains and surprisingly sudden falls of snow, while prowling, hungry coyotes and mountain lion posed a danger.

He recalled how, in his family's time, the supplies kept at the cabin included basic medical equipment. He wondered if such was still the custom with the MC now absorbed into the Slanted B. He badly needed to attend to the bullet slash in his arm and Brimstone was closed to him. At this time of year, the line cabin should be untenanted. In his current dilemma, a venture on to the hostile territory of the Brix empire in search of aid for his injury seemed to be his only course. He decided that, hazardous though it was, he'd take the chance.

Cautiously, he rose, coaxed the bronc to its feet, mounted and, still keeping his head below the high scrub, put distance between himself and Brimstone.

He hit open country with the town beyond the horizon, pushed the bronc onward, found a small stream where he rested and allowed the animal to drink. An examination of his wound showed an angry but superficial tear in the flesh, rimmed with now drying blood.

'Not so bad as I thought but it still needs dressing,' he told himself as he sloshed water around the injury.

He resumed the ride, negotiated the rock-studded old watercourse and eventually emerged on the furthest northern fringe of the old MC ranges. He felt an emotional tug at being on land familiar from his boyhood which was now possessed by the grasping owner of the Slanted B. Here, the terrain was greener, some of the best graze in Tinkettle Basin, and there were folds of land, some of them crowned with live-oak groves. Clennan crested such a hump and saw the cabin nestling in the hollow below him.

Two unsaddled horses grazed in the small corral beside the cabin. 'Blast it! The place isn't empty!' he growled to the horse. 'Looks like there's two in there.'

He saw, too, a rider, approaching the small structure who was near enough to be recognized as the slimmer and lighter of the pair he had humiliated by taking their saddles and weapons. The horseman was making directly for the line cabin and was close upon it.

Clennan pulled his mount to a halt in the cover of a live-oak stand and watched the man close the distance between himself and the cabin, Then the rider's voice carried on the still air as he bellowed a message: 'Hello, the line cabin! Snead and Barnard! Get back to headquarters! Boss's orders!'

Then he recalled how Brix, with his acquisitive grasper's jealousy, seemed to keep his holdings under guard, as witnessed by his having a pair to ride the ridge trail which was not even part of Slanted B land. So a pair of his gunhawks were planted out here on the northern perimeter of his ill-acquired territory.

A figure in range garb appeared in the door of the cabin and yelled back at the approaching rider: 'What? What're you saying?'

The response hit Lew Clennan like a blow, sending a chill through his innards.

'Get back to headquarters!' shouted the approaching rider. 'You're needed. The Old Man is fixing up a party to raid the old Swede who runs the horse ranch yonder tonight. Seems the Swede is tied up with Lew Clennan. Saddle up and ride!'

A cold fury gripped Clennan as he had a vision of a horde of Slanted B gunsharps descending on Lars Lundgren's cabin to attack a lone man. He knew that the ruffians on Brix's payroll would not be above murdering the old horse rancher in his bed.

From his concealed position in the oaks he watched the rider draw closer to the cabin and saw a second man emerged from the door. At that point, his bronc was moved by some perverse instinct, probably induced by the animal's having endured long spells of enforced travelling, the possible scent of plentiful water nearby at the cabin or the proximity of three more horses.

The animal suddenly whinnied and bucked upward, causing Clennan's body to rise high in the saddle and so to become momentarily visible over the screening of brush which concealed him within the grove. The bronc bucked again, almost throwing its rider and making it difficult for Clennan to control the animal with only one fully functioning arm.

Corey Blivens, spurring his mount towards the cabin, heard the sharp, braying whinny of the animal, swung his head towards the sound and had a fleeting glimpse of the man in the trees. It was enough to permit certain points to register: the man was the wanted Clennan, he who had humiliated Blivens and his companion, and there was a splotch of blood on his left sleeve which suggested he was at a disadvantage on a decidedly fractious horse.

Blivens's intellect was not of the sharpest. He was little more than a yokel with a vicious streak who aspired to the dubious honours of a hardcase gunslick, and he now experienced a vicious desire for vengeance for the way Clennan made Jesse Coote and himself eat humble pie on the ridge trail. It overrode even the prospect of netting a reward for the capture of Clennan.

For Clennan was plainly there for the killing, with an injured arm and disadvantaged by a spooked horse. Thirsty for revenge, Blivens unholstered his Colt, swerved his horse and sent it charging up the hump topped by the grove where Clennan was fighting to control his bronc.

'*It's him! It's Clennan!*' he bellowed over his shoulder in the direction of the cabin.

About half-way up the rise he triggered a shot, but Clennan had swung low in the saddle in reaction to the prancing of the horse and the bullet screeched over his head, missing it by inches.

Clennan's bullet-bitten left arm was stiffening. He tried to stay in the saddle, gripping the sides of his mount with his knees as he drew his six-gun with his right hand. He saw the mounted Blivens now coming at him head on, snarling and panting, levelling his gun directly into his face. Clennan fired first as his animal lurched to one side. A lurid scarlet blotch suddenly appeared on Blivens's forehead an instant before he pitched backwards in the saddle, flinging his arms up to the sky and hurling his weapon away.

In the echo of the gunfire, the disturbed bronc bucked yet again and Clennan, not holding any controlling rein, was thrown out of the saddle.

He landed on his uninjured side, sprawling into the earth and losing his grip on his own handgun. He rolled, winded, and had an inverted view of two figures, running up the rise towards him – the Brix hardcases from the line cabin, both flourishing revolvers and with faces twisted into masks of fury.

Then his vision was momentarily obscured by Blivens's horse, bearing the slack corpse of the Slanted B rider, matching his own animal, jittering and prancing in startled response to the sudden blast of firing.

For an instant, the world seemed to stop and he felt the certainty of imminent death delivered from the guns of the two Slanted B men, lunging forward on his position. Just as Blivens's spooked horse danced out of the way, clearing his field of vision, he found his gun on the ground, then a second one – that flung away by the dying Blivens. He grabbed them, rolled over on his belly and fired both weapons simultaneously, desperately and point blank at the Slanted B pair now close upon him.

One gave a gurgling sigh and, through swirling gunsmoke, Clennan had a glimpse of both figures dropping to the ground, lifeless. He hugged the earth, gasping and hearing the restless movements of the scared horses. Then he came to his feet slowly. The humped bodies of the two men lay only a couple of yards from him and a third corpse was slumped over the saddle horn of the restless horse. His own bronc had moved some distance away but both animals were now less nervous.

Clennan felt a chill at his innards. He had taken three lives in a brief storm of furious action – the lives of men who were out to kill him. He had preserved his own life but he found guilt and horror in it rather than any sense of triumph.

It had happened on land which he considered to be still his – land to which his father once brought a young bride and which his father, his brothers and he had striven to build into a profitable cattle spread. He was jarred out of an encroaching sense of having defiled the soil into which the Clennans had settled their roots by a vivid recollection of what the horseman he killed had yelled to the two at the cabin.

A set of Eli Brix's night raiders were about to attack old Lars Ludgren, alone on his horse ranch!

He had to do something about it.

CHAPTER SEVEN

RAIDERS IN THE NIGHT

As hastily as he could, Clennan busied himself to bring some order to the scene in the grove of live-oaks after the shooting affray. Trying to disregard the pain of the bullet-slash in his arm, he caught the horse bearing the grisly burden of its dead rider, unhooked the man's boots from the stirrups and laid the corpse on the ground. He unsaddled the animal, still quivering with nervousness, removed its saddle and the accompanying blanket and range-trappings, including rifle and scabbard, and placed them beside the corpse. He slapped the rump of the animal and let it run loose. Next, he dragged the pair who had attacked him on foot from where they had fallen and stretched them alongside their companion.

With the next day's climbing sun, desert

115

buzzards would be attracted to the skies above this spot, alerting such Slanted B personnel as might be within sight to the presence of the corpses. They might then be afforded such niceties of ritual burial as someone thought fit. The loose horse would graze free and probably drift by instinct towards the ranch headquarters.

Although this location was far from the nerve centre of Brix's operations, there was a chance that other Slanted B riders were near enough to have heard the shooting and so come to investigate. He was all too aware that he would have to work fast to achieve the object of his coming here in the first place.

And, all the time, there was the gnawing consciousness of time ticking away, of the sun lowering in the sky and of a plot to attack old Lars when night fell.

Plainly, Brix's murderous mind had hatched another vengeful move and, just as plainly, it was spurred by Lars's association with Clennan. For the rider who alerted the two at the cabin had called: '*Seems the Swede is tied up with Lew Clennan. Saddle up and ride!*' Impelled by the need for urgent action, he collected his bronc, which had now found its nerve again, led it at a walk out of the grove and down the hump towards the cabin. He tethered the animal to the pole fence of the corral containing the two unsaddled horses and entered the cabin.

The place was untidy and none too clean, with tumbled clothing littering its couple of bunks and the remnants of a meal left on the rough boarded table, but the layout was the same as Clennan remembered it. The small cabinet he recollected was still fixed to the wall beside the window, and in it he found a roll of bandage and a large bottle of iodine, pretty well undisturbed from the old days of MC ownership. At the makeshift sink there was the usual big pitcher of fresh water.

Clennan worked as fast as he could with one fully functioning arm. The wound was superficial and it had ceased to bleed. He cleaned off the dried blood, washed the bullet-slash as thoroughly as he could, then endured the harsh bite of a liberal application of iodine. He bandaged the wound, making it an efficient and secure job if not a neat one.

He set about replenishing the chambers of his Colt and assuaged the hunger which now made itself felt, cramming into his mouth some of the scarcely fresh but still edible bread from the table. Then he drank the last of the water in the pitcher.

Outside, he allowed his bronc to continue cropping the grass sprouting around the corral for a brief spell, then led it into the corral to allow it to drink at the zinc trough in a corner of the structure. He left the corral gate open to allow the two Slanted B animals to wander out and graze free when it pleased them.

He considered the westering sun and tried to position himself mentally in relation to Lars's outfit. He was on highly dangerous ground, which Brix had claimed as his, and there was every chance of his encountering Slanted B riders, but if he rode as swiftly as he could on the fringe of this old MC region, he could reach the ridge trail which would bring him down to Lundgren's horse ranch somewhere around nightfall. It was his only chance of helping the old family friend in the face of Brix's crew of ruffians.

He set off, riding at a pace that would not overly strain his already tired bronc, covering the old MC land with an intensified determination to bring back his family's brand to this spread of Tinkettle Basin. Remembering his encounter with Ted Orme and Orme's revelation that he knew the whereabouts of the various members of the old crew who had drifted away, he vowed anew that he would break Brix's grip on the basin, take back the Clennan holdings and reassemble the set of wranglers who had worked the outfit with his father and brothers.

But first he had to push his war against the power of the Slanted B – and he was now on the prod, plunging once more into something in which the odds were stacked high against him.

Lars Lundgren had not weathered years on the bleak ranges of the north, including his involvement in the cattle wars, without becoming sensitive to signs and indications of trouble to come. Such sensitivity was a necessity of frontier life whether up north or down here on the border with Mexico.

This sixth sense caused him to look to his weapons when Lew Clennan showed up again. In view of the recent history of the Clennan family and knowing Lew's temperament and reputation, it was a sure thing that the prodigal's return to the basin would bring trouble.

Lars now had his six-gun and shell-belt ready to hand, likewise his fully charged Winchester while a bandoleer heavy with ammunition was hanging on a convenient hook on the wall.

'Let 'em come here and they'll get more than they bargained for,' he muttered to himself as he looked out of the window yet another time into the gathering dusk.

The fact was that Lars was expecting a reaction to the ruse he had worked with the Trilling operatives. He had long ago reasoned that while Clennan made no mention of where he was headed after leaving the horse ranch, the only track he could logically take was the ridge trail. He would certainly avoid any which would lead him into the heart of Eli Brix's holdings, nor would he take any of the others, which would take him to the desert flats. Therefore, for reasons known only to himself, Clennan had gone up the ridge trail towards the tableland above the basin. Lars had thrown the Trilling pair off Lew's trail for a time and he still chuckled at the way they fell for the act he put on when they stopped off at his place.

While he found pleasure in the notion of the pair being stranded at nightfall on the margin of inhospitable and waterless terrain, he knew there was every chance of their coming out of that predicament by traversing Slanted B land and the possibility of Brix and his men learning from them that Lew Clennan was in the region for sure. There could be repercussions against himself.

Lars was thankful that advancing years and the edgy life he had always led had robbed him of a need for much sleep. He was alert and prepared, keeping a watch from his window. He intended to defend his place; nevertheless, his spirited little pony was ready, saddled and tethered by the rear door in case he had to make a hasty retreat if the situation became too hot.

Lars's instincts enabled him to predict the future course of events with uncanny accuracy. Retribution was now boiling at the headquarters of the Slanted B. The setting sun was splashing the wide desert skies with garish crimson and gold, and gun-heavy men were saddling and mounting their horses. Eli Brix had taken an unusual decision. He usually sent his crew out to do his dirty work, captained by his foreman, the loutish Abe Gawley, but this was one raiding party he intended to head himself. He had two Navy Colts buckled under his respectable black coat and he sat his saddle with his heavy beard thrust pugnaciously forward, looking like a general about to launch an action which could decide the course of a war.

Lew Clennan was somewhere in the vicinity. Brix was sure that Lars Lundgren knew something about him and he had by now formed the notion that Clennan might be holed up at the old Swede's place.

Clennan meant trouble and Brix had a murderous yearning to find him. If he was not at the horse ranch then Lundgren probably knew where he was and Brix aimed to force that information out of the horse rancher. He'd make the boys push this matter to a conclusion favourable to himself and, if it came to it, one more corpse and one more burned-out place was of little account to the would-be emperor of Tinkettle Basin.

There was a last-minute impatient clattering of hoofs, rattling of ringbits, creaking of leather and a shucking on of bandoleers and carbines amid the growl of harsh voices as the raiding party readied itself to ride out.

'Damned if I know what's happened to Snead and Barnard from the line camp and that new guy I sent for them,' snarled Brix to Gawley, saddled up beside him. 'We've waited long enough for them and if they can't jump to an order, they'll answer to me for it later. C'mon, let's ride!'

The string of horsemen trooped out of the Slanted B yard, hard-eyed and with mouths set in cruel, determined lines into the gathering night.

It was full night when they approached Lars Lundgren's ranch and Lars, prodded by that instinct for sniffing trouble in the offing which was honed by his exploits up north, was sitting by his window, with a cocked six-gun in his hand in readiness.

'I just knew it,' he commented as he heard the tramp of horses nearing his ranch yard. 'Just knew I'd have guests from the Slanted B tonight. Well, I'm not so blamed old I don't relish a fight – even with the odds stacked against me!'

In the night-shrouded yard, he saw the silhouettes of mounted men emerging from the shadows, clattering in like an invading army. Lars's resolve held firm though he knew of Brix's vicious activities since coming to Tinkettle Basin, with the killings of the Clennans, father and sons, and the depredations against Harry Siggs's little outfit where Brix now mined silver.

Eli Brix's harsh voice bawled: 'Lundgren! Step out here – I want to talk to you!'

Lars put his mouth against the thick glass of the window. 'Get the hell off my land!' he bellowed.

The dark mass of riders out in the yard thickened, making Lars realize how many of them were crowding in on him. As they drew nearer, he discerned the figures of some he knew well as the strutting Brix men so frequently found throwing their weight around in Brimstone and its vicinity, the likes of Abe Gawley, ever present at his boss's side and Switzer and Dutton, veterans among the Slanted B's ruffians, signed on for trigger money.

Hell, he has the whole ugly bunch with him and all spoiling for a fight but I'm damned if I'll knuckle down to them, thought Lars.

One among the mounted crew was hardly spoiling for a fight, however. He was Jesse Coote, a newcomer to the Slanted B strength with his trail-partner, Corey Blivens. Blivens had been detailed to fetch the two manning the far line cabin but they had not shown up and Coote had been swallowed into this big raiding party without having any say in the matter. He was uneasy about the whole project, just as he and Blivens were uneasy about having thrown in with Brix and the Slanted B in the first place. They considered themselves to be tough but found they did not match up to the hardened villainy typifying the outfit's payroll.

Then there was the matter of the private deal he and Blivens imagined they had struck with the two Trilling men. Brix wanted to deal with Lew Clennan in his own brutal way and if he and his crew got to him first, there would be no hope of Coote and Blivens collecting a cut of the reward they so fondly hoped for. Coote was an uncomfortable saddle-mate to the collection of ruffians now menacing old Lars Lundgren. If he had his way, he would be clear of the Slanted B and, in partnership with Blivens, be engaged in tracking Clennan in search of the promised portion of the reward.

Coote watched uneasily as Brix spurred his horse a little closer to Lundgren's cabin, then shouted: 'You know something about Clennan, Lundgren! He came here to make trouble for me and I want him. If he's in there with you, I want him, pronto. Open up, damn you, or I'll wreck your place!'

Lars had no illusions concerning Brix's lawless capabilities. The old Swede had put a good portion of his later years into building up his horse-ranching operation and his corrals were full of valuable stock. Brix would have no compunction about wreaking mayhem on the whole enterprise. Lars had much to lose and Brix was pushing him into a tight corner but his engrained, dogged fighting spirit would not yield. He placed his mouth close to the window again and roared: 'Go to hell, Brix! Take yourself and your scum off my place!'

'You damned old fool! Open up or suffer the consequences!' roared Brix. He waved both Navy Colts in the air, then levelled one at the cabin and fired a warning shot, sending lead thudding into the stout log wall.

This was precisely what was required to provoke Lars Ludgren to decisive action to defend his property. He smashed the window with the barrel of his six-gun, levelled the weapon through the hole and triggered a shot at the mounted Brix who made a big silhouette of a target to the fore of his raiding party. It was aimed deliberately over the rancher's head and the bullet's close proximity caused Brix to duck, cursing into his beard.

'The next one will be meant to hit!' hooted Lars. 'I can drop damn near all of you from here before you get a chance to finish me. Get the hell back to where you came from!'

'You old fool,' responded Brix. 'Can't you see you're outnumbered?'

At the rancher's elbow, Abe Gawley, his foreman, growled: 'Run his stock off, Mr Brix. It's all good horseflesh. Let's run those cayuses off to our place.'

'Sure,' spat Brix, his dark eyes glittering vindictively. 'We'll run his horseflesh off – *but, first, we'll burn him out!*'

CHAPTER EIGHT

EXPLOSION!

Nightfall found Clennan coming off the Slanted B land which had once been in MC ownership where it fringed the lower reaches of the ridge trail. He had traversed the hostile terrain without further incident and followed the ridge trail to where it petered away from the shoulder of the ridge, giving way to open country. His obvious move was a circling ride to bring him down sloping terrain and approach Lars Lundgren's place from the rear. This elevated land behind the horse ranch might give him some chance of viewing what was happening there, so far as was possible on a night which had only a fugitive moon, visible now and again with the clearing of scudding clouds.

That something was happening at the ranch was made evident well before he had any sight of it. The blasting of shots and a whooping and roaring of harsh voices and the neighing and braying of disturbed horses came echoing over the ridges of the land. Clennan pressed the bronc onward up a rise and saw below him a garish flaring of fire and the vivid flashes of muzzle-flames from weapons. Smoke plumed up into the night sky and the slight breeze carried the acrid smell of burning wood towards him.

'Damn it, horse, they're burning him out!' he snorted to his mount as he pulled rein on the downward slope to assess the situation below. From what he could see, a sizeable raiding party was going a fair way to laying waste to Lars Lundgren's place and his fear was that the old Swede was already dead.

He drew his Colt and took the bronc at a cautious walk down the slanted land, heading towards the scene of mayhem below. Then his finger tightened on the trigger as he saw a dark shape moving up the slope towards him. It resolved itself into a horse and rider, moving through the darkness almost furtively.

Clennan screwed his eyes to pierce the darkness as the horseman approached. He recognized the rider as one of the pair whom he had encountered on the ridge trail, the man whose companion he had left as a corpse in the grove. The man recognised him and saw the pistol which Clennan levelled directly at his head. Startled and wide-eyed, he reined his mount to a halt.

'Don't shoot,' he mouthed, throwing up his hands. 'I'm getting the hell out of it. I haven't the guts for what's going on down there.'

'What *is* going on down there?' demanded Clennan icily.

'They've set the old Swede's place afire and he's in there, shooting it out,' said Jesse Coote. 'They'll kill the old man for sure but I'm damned if I want any part of it. I'm sneaking away. I'm not lily-livered but Brix's way of doing things is too much for me.'

Coote was face to face with the man for whose capture he hoped to net a portion of the reward on the dubious say-so of Reeder and Corkery, but that consideration had now dissolved. He was of a mind to put Tinkettle Basin and all connected with it well behind him.

'You're wise,' said Clennan, still keeping his six-gun levelled. 'Keep riding and don't bother looking for the guy you had with you when we met before. I let daylight into him.'

Coote's mouth slackened. 'You mean you—'

'I mean he tried to kill me and got killed instead.' He nodded a backward gesture, dismissing Coote to ride away. 'Get the hell out of here and don't turn around and try to backshoot me when you go or I'll drop you too.'

He twisted around in the saddle and kept his Colt square on the departing rider as he took his mount up the slope to be gathered into darkness.

Yet thicker smoke was drifting up from the violent scene below the slanted terrain and Clennan, spurred by anxiety for Lars, rode quickly but cautiously down into the foggy clouds towards the rear of the cabin.

He came to the fringe of a fury of action within a fiery chaos, the flames of which painted highlights on a grotesque drama of plunging, rearing horsemen who loosed shots at the cabin. To one side, through scarves of smoke, he saw that the gates of the horse corrals had been opened and Slanted B riders were running off Lars's stock, the panicky animals neighing in protest as they shied away from the flames from the cabin.

The fog of smoke offered some cover at the rear of the cabin and, unnoticed by the raiders, Clennan rode boldly towards the building, covering his lower face with his kerchief. He swerved the bronc towards the rear door of the cabin, where he saw Lars's saddled and tethered pony, plunging in fear. Already, flames were licking over the roof and he guessed that a good portion of the front of the building must be on fire. He could hear shots being repeatedly fired from inside the cabin.

Hell, he thought, *the tough old buzzard is still in there and still shooting at the bunch at the front of the place with the whole caboodle ready to go up like matchwood any second!*

The sharp bark of the carbine echoed out of the cabin again and again, indicating that Lars was somehow standing his ground though the interior of the building must be filled with choking smoke. Clennan wanted to crash through the closed, and probably locked, rear door and haul the old Swede out physically, but he dare not leave the saddle since, in the blazing, smoky turmoil, his bronc would be sure to panic and run if not controlled.

129

Keeping himself slumped forward in the saddle and cloaked by the smoke, Clennan was still unspotted by Brix's men who were busy hoorawing the stock of horseflesh out of the corrals, though the smoky chaos of their own making was causing them to splutter and cough. He rode to within a foot of the rear door and was about to cast caution to the wind, leap from his mount and make an attempt to charge in and rescue Lars before he was overcome by smoke and fire when the door burst open. Followed by a banner of sparks and smoke, still clutching his Winchester and with a bandoleer of ammunition across his chest, Lars Lundgren came stumbling out, coughing and gasping. Shrouded by swirling smoke, he was totally unnoticed by the raiders at the rear of the cabin who were giving themselves to horse-theft.

Lars stood for a moment, his chest heaving for breath. Clennan yelled at him from behind the mask of his kerchief: 'Lars! Get on your cayuse and ride!'

Lars looked at him through the swirls of smoke. He saw a rider on a plunging bronc, a man whose lower face was covered and whom he at first took to be one of Brix's raiders. He made a menacing gesture with his Winchester.

'Dammit, Lars, it's me – Lew!' roared Clennan. 'Ride while the going's good!'

'Lew!' gasped Lars hoarsely. 'How the hell. . . ?'

'*Ride*!' repeated Clennan.

Lars, with surprising alacrity and still gripping his Winchester, made a one-handed grab at the rein of his jumpy pony, untethered the animal and swung into the saddle.

'Ride for the high country,' instructed Clennan.

'I don't like leaving these hellions to—' began Lars.

'It's too late to save anything here. Let's get the hell out quick,' urged Clennan, spurring his bronc. With relief, he saw that Lars was wheeling his horse to follow him.

The masking fog gave them cover enough to ride away from the rear of the cabin and make for the ridge trail which would take them well away from the Brix-dominated region of Tinkettle Basin. They had almost made a clean getaway, then a voice suddenly hooted from the midst of the men clearing the corrals of stock: '*Hey – the old-timer's getting away! Somebody's with him! I reckon it's Clennan!*' A shot followed, fired randomly out of the smoke and Clennan instinctively turned and fired back. In doing so, he had a glimpse of Lars Lundgren's cabin, now becoming a crackling and spitting inferno, with a confusion of men and horses boiling around it.

Another voice rose above the din: '*Lundgren and Clennan are getting away, Mr Brix!*'

Then came a throaty roar from Eli Brix: '*Get after them!*'

As the two galloped out of the confusion into clearer air, they heard wild activity in their wake as some of the raiders tried to control their fire-panicked horses and give chase. Clear of the fire, they were cloaked by darkness and they plunged across open country to the point where the ridge trail started its upward slant and swerved on to it.

Lars's pony was fresher than Clennan's bronc, which had endured a gruelling day's wayfaring and was now beginning to show distinct signs of becoming jaded. In the fugitives' backtrail there was an ominous drumming of horses, growing louder.

Clennan and Lars toiled up the trail, forcing energy out of their mounts, though Clennan had doubts about the staying power of his bronc.

Behind them, Eli Brix, in a temper blazing as furiously as Lars's cabin, had forced his animal to the head of his men and was leading the pursuit, urging them on with torrents of profanity. Lew Clennan represented danger to him. He had considered his murderous double-dealings to secure the Clennan family's MC land to be a closed matter. Mark Clennan and his sons Frank and Ed were dead and the tempestuous youngest son had long disappeared from the scene, perhaps to have met the sort of frontier fate often visited on such hotheads. But the youngest Clennan had showed up again, with his thrusting, pugnacious temperament backed by a badman's reputation. So long as Lew Clennan was in Tinkettle Basin, there would be trouble for Eli Brix. The would-be emperor of the basin knew it and would not rest until the youngest Clennan was as dead as his father and brothers.

Now the infuriated Brix and his crew were hot in pursuit of Clennan and his doughty old companion, plunging through the darkness up the ridge trail, with the bloody-minded intention of ensuring that they did not get out of the basin alive. The horses of both parties snorted and steamed up the uncertain, slanted trail and Clennan was aware of the nagging bullet-slash in his arm and the heaving of his tired mount, while Lars, on his fresher pony, muttered and growled. It had never been in his nature to turn and run.

'Blast it, Lew, I feel like I'm running out on my life's work,' he complained. 'I should be standing and fighting.'

'Quit groaning. We're still ahead of them and we'll give them a fight yet,' answered Clennan, though he was privately anxious about the flagging stamina of his bronc. The pair pounded onward, their panting animals striving against the upward slant of the uncertain terrain beneath their feet.

The Slanted B riders came hard after them, led by the furious Brix and jostling two abreast on the narrow trail, on one side of which was the slope of the ridge and the gulf of Tinkettle Basin while, to the other, there was a rocky, boulder-studded slope which was almost a wall. Abruptly, the whole scene was lit by a flash of vivid light, quickly followed by a thundering reverberation from the southern end of the basin, somewhere beyond the Slanted B land. It sent echoes clattering across the wide land A vivid yellow and crimson glow flared against the night sky, highlighting for an instant the far line of hills towards the Mexican border.

'Explosion!' roared Abe Gawley, riding beside

Eli Brix. He reined his horse to a halt and looked back, bewildered. 'Some kind of explosion out yonder on our southern range!'

Eli Brix also halted his mount and the remainder of the party drew rein. All heads turned back to the source of the sudden blast.

'It's over towards the workings!' exclaimed Brix. 'Something's happened at my silver-workings!'

Out at the southern reaches of the land grasped by Brix, he ran his ore operation, with Mexicans and Indians providing the toil while a quartet of his gun-ruffians supplied what with some exaggeration might be called management skills. A mine had been developed in the rocky foothills of land once owned by Harry Siggs. It provided a good yield, lining Eli Brix's pockets yet further and Brix had every hope that it was only the first step in his creation of a widespread silver-mining enterprise to match his cattle-raising.

But something unexpected had occurred somewhere near the mine – something which sent this crashing blast across the vastness of Tinkettle Basin below the ridge like the opening of an artillery salvo.

The halted Slanted B riders made a jostling knot on the precarious trail, each man looking back in the direction of the blast. The diversion gave some advantage to Clennan and Lars, desperately forcing their lathered mounts onward.

'What the Sam Hill was that racket?' shouted Lars.

'Blamed if I know. Sounds like someone's

started a war,' responded Clennan. 'Keep moving, Lars. We might get the jump on them yet.'

A strategic move was forming itself in his mind as, in the darkness, he searched his memory of the geography of the trail. The dim sound of falling water ahead reassured and guided him and he forced his bronc onward towards it. They were approaching the little waterfall and the oasis at which he had stopped on his earlier journey along this trail. It was located on a bend on the narrow track where there were scattered boulders. It was a natural strong point where, even in darkness, two men positioned in the sheltering rocks could command the bend and fire on pursuers coming around it. A halt at that point also offered a chance to give their animals a breather.

He made out the dim contours of the scattered boulders and heard the water cascading down to its rocky basin beside the bend. Aware that the pursuers were briefly distracted by the faraway explosion and were now halted behind them, Clennan panted: 'Get behind the rocks. We can hold them off for a spell!'

Lars saw his chance of pursuing his preferred strategy of standing and fighting and spurred his mount into the rocks on his companion's tail. Clennan snatched his Winchester from its scabbard as he left his saddle and the two scrambled into the shelter of this position which commanded the trail. Their horses, heaving with exertion but now in a protected situation, instinctively made for the water.

The pair waited, screwing their eyes against the darkness, looking towards where the trail bent around an outcropping slightly below them. A tension-heavy silence was suddenly broken by the thump of toiling horses approaching the bend below as the chase was renewed. It grew nearer, then the pair behind the rocks fired simultaneously, sending their shots across the turn in the trail around which the pursuing horsemen were about to swing. Hot lead sang angrily close to the beard of the infuriated Eli Brix, well to the fore of his men.

The rancher drew rein, causing his horse to slither to a halt. He hauled the animal back from the bend where Clennan and Lars were positioned, pumping and firing their carbines. The riders stopped their horses abruptly, so that they tangled with each other in confusion.

'Get back from the bend!' hooted Brix. 'They're holed up somewhere in the rocks. Blast them out!' He fired his twin Colts in the direction of the muzzle-flashes coming from the fugitives' position.

And that was the signal for his crew, gathered into a defensive knot of men and animals, to loose a fusillade of lead towards Lew Clennan and his companion.

CHAPTER NINE

DYNAMITE

Bullets whanged in a brief, savage swarm around the position where Clennan and Lars were hunkered down behind the rocks, taking no effect because the location of those firing them, behind the hump of land and rocks at the bend in the trail, offered no realistic chance of accurate aim. The two fugitives crouched low and made cautious and sporadic appearances above the rim of their cover to fire answering shots in a mere token resistance which was wearing on their resources of lead.

'Damn it, we've got each other pretty near pinned down,' muttered Clennan. 'We can't keep this up until kingdom come. We've got to find a way of getting off this trail.'

'Where in hell are we running to, anyway?' asked Lars.

'Kimmins City, I have a cache of supplies and

ammunition there. They're the means of keeping ourselves alive for a spell. I know getting this bunch off our tails is a tall order but there are urgent things to do. Listen, if I don't get out of this and you do, I have a poke of money on me, drawn from my account at the bank. It's all legitimately mine. Take it. You've lost your place and horses. You'll need a fresh start.'

Clennan paused and grabbed his companion's sleeve.

He emphasized gravely: 'Most important of all, there's a document in the safe at the Brimstone bank that'll finish Brix. It's a confession about the bushwhackings of my old man and brothers and the crooked deals to grab the MC with Tait's help. I squeezed it out of Tait. Jeff Samson, the banker, wants to see Brix finished as much as we do and he'll be sure to give it to you. Get it to the US marshal's office in Tucson and be sure Wiseman and the so-called law in Brimstone don't get hold of it. I reckon there's enough in the paper to finish not only Brix but Horace Tait, for his part in it but I guess he's already pulled up his stakes and vamoosed. The genuine law will bring Brix to account if only that paper is put into to the hands of the US marshal.'

'By grab, that's music to my ears,' grinned Lars, filling the magazine of his Winchester from his bandoleer. 'But you're talking like a man making his will and I don't aim to see either of us finished off in this ruckus. If I do cash in my checks, I'll come back as a ghost to settle Brix's hash!' He

slithered up a sheltering rock on his belly and
fired a wild shot towards the Slanted B party. It was
at once answered by a couple of bullets, ill-aimed
because of the darkness and the disadvantaged
position of the holed-up Brix men.

Lew Clennan was acutely aware that this situation could become a total stalemate, so long as
ammunition held out, with each set of opponents
firing from their static positions without any
notable effect. It was uncomfortably plain, too,
that the Brix party had more men, more weapons
and, consequently a better supply of ammuntion.

Though Clennan and Lars commanded the
bend in the trail, holding back pursuit, this stand-
off could not last indefinitely, and now the first sliv-
ers of red dawn were beginning to streak the far
sky in the east.

There was a lull in the exchanges for a brief time
and the awakening dawn strengthened. Soon,
there would be full, bright desert-country daylight
across the whole terrain.

Then came the harsh bark of a rifle. Something
smote a rock up near the beginning of the spill of
the waterfall in the high slant of land above the
position held by Clennan and Lars. Then, with a
leaden thud, it bounced off a rock inches away
from Clennan's head, chipping a chunk out of it.
Another came, then another in rapid succession,
finding marks within inches of the two in the
rocks. The shots were diverted into their position,
after being aimed at a portion of the outcropping
above.

'Snap-shooting, damn it!' said Lars. 'They can't get direct aim on us but they've got a marksman among them whose getting at us by hitting that rock above us first.'

'Sure, and he's a pretty good snap-shooter, too. He's working blind and trying to hit us by luck, but it's nearly daylight and he could improve his aim,' replied Clennan, ducking as yet another deflected bullet smote part of their rocky fortifications. 'Sooner or later, he'll hit one of us or one of the horses – and it'll be worse if we fall asleep. We'll have to take a chance on making another run for it.'

Lars gave a philosophic grunt. 'OK by me. No point in both sides sitting around bottled up for ever. The horses are rested some and they've drunk their fill. Let's do it.'

The marksman down at the Slanted B's entrenched position was improving his touch and evidently enjoying himself. He sent sporadic shots spinning around his unseen targets as, bent almost double, they scrambled among the rocks to gather their animals from where they were cropping the sparse grass around the pool.

They mounted, spurred their animals out of the rock cluster and back on to the trail.

The light was strengthening now and the hurried clatter of the horses was carried to the Slanted B pursuers, sparking venomous profanities from Eli Brix.

'They're on the move again!' he snarled, jumping swiftly towards his horse, sheltered behind a boulder. 'This time we'll get them. C'mon – move!'

There was an immediate scramble by his men, who had been chafing under the experience of being pinned down at the bend in the trail with a fruitless expending of ammunition, firing at a position almost impossible to hit. They were quickly in their saddles and back on the trail, stirring the dust in the wake of the pair who were once more tackling the upward rise of the ridge trail.

Clennan and Lars, crouched over their saddle horns and spurring their mounts furiously, at least had the advantage of freshly watered horses, whereas the Slanted B party had been pinned done in a dry location and their animals were now wheezing and toiling. Eli Brix was to the fore of them with one hand grasping the rein and the other waving one of his twin six-guns. He triggered off a couple of shots made ineffectual by the jogging of his horse over the trail's irregular surface. Nevertheless, they screeched through the air just above the madly riding, crouching pair.

They took yet another bend where the trail snaked around the shoulder of land to its right. To the left was the dizzy drop of the ridge and, below it, the broad expanse of Tinkettle Basin, now washed by the bright light of a new day. Ahead, above the rising trail, they could see the tableland and, with eyes narrowed against the brightness of the sun, Clennan discerned the dim outlines of the woebegone abandoned structures of Kimmins City.

The two sets of horsemen were now approaching the top of the trail, where it flattened out and met the broad expanse of the country above the basin. The Slanted B riders kept tenaciously on the tails of Clennan and Lars, who now put on an energetic spurt to ride clear of the narrow confines of the trail and gain the more spacious land. Their more refreshed horses gave them a slight advantage and the gap between the two galloping parties widened a little.

Now, at the extreme summit of the trail, with the rim of Tinkettle Basin lying behind them, Clennan and Lundgren found a bewildering scene unfolding in front of them. In a cloud of hoof-stirred dust, a knot of riders were pounding at top speed towards them from the direction of the ghost settlement of Kimmins City. In the fog of dust, they discerned wide-brimmed Mexican sombreros and flourished carbines approaching them.

The troop of riders pounded into the path of Clennan and Lars. They pulled rein and halted their animals, causing the pair to also yank leather, bringing their mounts to a sliding stop, with Eli Brix and his crew behind them still thundering up to the top of the trail.

Then something was sent spinning through the air from the squad of wide-hatted intruders. With a whirring sound, it sailed over the heads of Clennan and Lars, leaving behind a thin string of smoke. It landed in the gap between the pair and their pursuers. Then came a vivid white flash and an ear-splitting crack. Clennan and Lars felt the explosion as a severe thump in the back. They were momentarily robbed of breath and their mounts were sent skittering forward, but the Slanted B riders took its full force. It blew them back in a falling confusion of men and animals.

Clennan and Lars managed to keep in their saddles and, with breath gusted from their lungs, they fought to control their fractious animals in a fog of dust and smoke. Looking back, they saw that the explosion had wrought a dire effect on those who had pursued them. Men and horses made humped and motionless shapes on the trail into which a sizeable crater had been blown.

'Dynamite!' spluttered Lars. 'That was dynamite!'

Now, they became aware that some of the figures in the costume of Mexican peons were dismounting and walking purposefully and silently to form what amounted to a guard between themselves and the shambles of Eli Brix's crew.

'*Sí, señor.* Dynamite, placed with accuracy and revolutionary fervour where it could do most good,' said a gruff voice behind Clennan and Lars.

Turning, Clennan saw, to the fore of the Mexicans, a figure in serape and sombrero, the brim of which shaded dark Indian eyes. A carbine protruded from the folds of his serape.

'Who might you be?' asked Clennan, still bewildered by the rapid and unexpected turn of events.

Another figure stepped out from the line of men, slender and boyish, in faded jeans, shirt and a broad-brimmed hat and bearing a businesslike Winchester; a figure which stated:

143

'He's Nacio – just Nacio. If the Yaqui had aristocracy, he'd be aristocracy and he's a man of many skills, one of which you've just experienced: the use of the most effective element of warfare – surprise. Good morning, Mr Clennan and friend.' The voice was steady, firm – and feminine.

Lew Clennan blinked dust from his eyes and stared. Under the wide brim of the hat, he saw an attractive, dusty and determined face, softening into a smile which held more than a suggestion of impishness.

This was the girl who had held him at carbine-point in Kimmins City.

CHAPTER TEN

RECKONING

Where the ridge trail met the wide land spreading above Tinkettle Basin, dust was settling over the after-effects of the explosion. There was a tangled sprawl of men and horses littering the ground. Some were plainly stilled in death, while others were stirring, coming to their feet, shocked, shaking, coughing and showing no inclination to fight.

The Mexicans spread themselves to make a barrier between the Slanted B men and Clennan, Lars and the girl, with their weapons levelled menacingly as stillness descended on the scene.

Then, from the fogged swirls of smoke and dust, lurching forward unsteadily, dishevelled but still powerfully impressive in his height, with his beard jutting in pugnacious defiance and with a Navy Colt gripped in each hand, came Eli Brix. He fronted the shambles of his crew and glared wide-eyed at the array of enemies before him.

Lew Clennan came speedily out of his saddle, Colt in hand. He was aching for sleep and the wound in his arm was nagging but a surge of vengeful energy revitalized him. The man responsible for the murders of his father and brothers and grabbing the MC spread was still alive, still clutching his two six-guns and only yards away. Brix was doubly armed in the face of Clennan's single weapon but Clennan's old tempestuousness took over and he knew only a blazing lust to settle the bill which had brought the prodigal back to Tinkettle Basin.

He thrust himself through the line of Mexicans, stood squarely in front of Brix. 'By God, Brix, I'm going to kill you here and now!' he bellowed. 'You know me – Lew Clennan – and you know why I'm going to blast you to hell and gone.'

There was a moment of tight tension in which the pair faced each other, glowering. Then it was broken by the firmly determined voice of the girl who had also pushed herself before the line of Mexicans and now stood brandishing her Winchester.

'Hold it! I want my say!' she called. 'I want you to know how well and truly finished you are, Brix. You're no longer in the silver-mining business. Your workings were blown sky-high by my friends last night. Oh, the unfortunates who were exploited by you in the mine and the specimens who were in charge of them were taken to safety first, but your workings were blown to dust.'

Now, to both Clennan and Lars, there returned

the memory of the shattering explosion heard across the basin during the chase in the night. Each reflected in his own way that, when it came to decisive generalship, this slender girl was gifted in spades.

Brix was standing transfixed, glaring at the girl with his mouth open.

'Who the hell are you, girl?' he growled hoarsely.

'Daphne Siggs, that's who,' she answered. 'Nice name, isn't it? Pretty and ladylike. Well, don't be fooled by it. I know you've never heard of me but I've been laying plans for a long time to make you hear *from* me. You ran my old man off his place and grabbed his land because you got the whiff of a valuable silver-seam there. He's dead now. You broke him and he up and died and I'm out to make you pay.'

Brix took another step forward. His face contorted in fury as he looked first at Clennan, then the girl. He stood on shaking legs for a moment, dazed and yet just about able to take in that he stood in the mangled shambles of men and horses which also represented the ruination of his enterprise in Tinkettle Basin. The expertly tossed stick of fused dynamite which had exploded fully in front of his pursuing horsemen but behind the backs of Clennan and Lundgren had wrought severe damage. Several of his most vicious henchmen were plainly dead, among them Dutton and Switzer. Others were injured, some writhing in the dust and others trying to come to their senses.

147

But Brix still gripped his pair of Navy Colts, pointed at the moment at the ground. He found his balance and drew himself up to his full height. Briefly, with his hefty stature and the kind of beard which, in statesmen and generals, betokened authority, he almost looked impressive. He plainly knew the game was up but there was a wild fanaticism in his eyes – and a light of last-ditch desperation.

He worked his mouth into a sneer.

'And the pair of you want satisfaction do you?' he snarled. 'Yes, Clennan, I made sure I got hold of the MC graze by my own means – and I'm the man who organized what were good enough ends for your old man and your brothers. It was done the way we did things back in the grass wars up north and to hell with mealy-mouthed talk about fair and square dealings. As for you, girl, yes, I ran your old man off his place and turned his glorified dirt farm into a proposition that paid me plenty.' He spat into the dirt, then swiftly raised and levelled his two Colts point blank, one at Clennan and the other at Daphne Siggs. '*So be damned to both of you!*' he bellowed.

But his face had telegraphed his intention a split second before he made his move and Clennan charged forward, his gun bucking and blasting in his hand. Brix gave a gurgling cry and pitched forwards with his arms flailing upwards like those of a drowning man being swallowed by ocean waves. He discharged both Navy Colts into the sky simultaneously.

Clennan's desperate charge caused him to lose his footing and trip immediately after he fired. He hit the dust face down and rolled over, then saw, lurching out of fogs of cordite smoke just behind the dead form of the would-be emperor of the basin, the squat, simian figure of Brix's foremen, Abe Gawley. His blocky face was a mask of vengeful hatred and he was lumbering forward, bearing down on the sprawling Clennan, levelling a six-gun at his head and about to squeeze the trigger.

'*Gawley, you fat sidewinder – I owe you this!*' roared a familiar voice from near the line of Mexicans.

Gawley looked up for an instant, at which point a carbine blasted and a shell screamed over the figure of Clennan, lying in the dust. Abruptly, Gawley's mouth fell wide open. He dropped his revolver, then crumpled in a heap, falling across the corpse of Eli Brix.

Clennan propped himself up on his elbows and saw Lars Lundgren, still in his saddle, gripping his Winchester from the mouth of which blue smoke dribbled.

Lars gave Clennan a satisfied grin. 'I owed him something for what he and the whole damned bunch of 'em did to my place,' he called.

Clennan came up from the ground. 'Thanks, Lars. He damned near finished me', he said, spitting dust.

Lars grunted. 'Think nothing of it. I owed you a favour, too.'

Clennan faced the wounded and battered remnants of the Slanted B crew, all now totally beaten and frozen under the threatening guns of Daphne Siggs and her Mexican colleagues.

'You're all through with Tinkettle Basin,' he roared hoarsely. 'Brix is dead, the Slanted B is finished and there's no one to pay your gun-wages. You have nothing to gain and everything to lose. I have proof of Brix's devilry all tucked away in a safe place and ready to be presented to the US Marshal in Tucson. If things go the full distance, there could be the hangrope for some of you and the penitentiary for others. The odds are stacked against you if you figure you can try what Brix and Gawley just tried.'

To a man, what was left of Eli Brix's outfit considered the line of heavily armed Mexicans confronting them, with the belligerent girl and the mounted Lundgen, both toting Winchesters, to their fore. The Mexicans' grim faces, blackened by the sun, seamed by exposure to harsh weathers and deprivation and ornamented by drooping moustaches, were utterly without mercy.

Clennan jerked his head towards the girl. 'Of course, this young lady might be in favour of marching the whole boiling of you off to face justice,' he declared. 'Or maybe she'll be content to see you vamoose for the border, with a good chance of the US Marshals eventually catching up with you, waving warrants. That's a fairer deal than Brix and the Slanted B ever gave anyone by a damnsight.'

Daphne Siggs considered the defeated crew disdainfully. 'Let them bury their dead and ride off

150

to hell and gone,' she said. 'Brix is gone and that's plenty good enough for me.' She made for her horse and Clennan trudged towards his bronc.

'Some darned woman!' he enthused. 'A specialist with dynamite and general of her own private army which seems to have invaded from Mexico!'

'I'm more than that,' she said, climbing into her saddle. 'I'm also a qualified nurse and that dried blood on your sleeve tells me you have a wound needing attention. C'mon.'

The mingled aroma of *tamales*, coffee and *cigarillo* smoke filled the air of the large cave dug out by desperate silver-hounds at the rear of Kimmins City. The Mexicans were sitting around, taking their ease, and Lars Lundgren was satisfying his hunger. Daphne Siggs, with a professional chest of medical supplies, was cleaning up Lew Clennan's makeshift attempt at dressing his wound.

'It beats me,' he said. 'I figured I'd blundered into something soon after I came to Kimmins City, but I never imagined you had an army and a supply base with horses and dynamite established here.'

'It took some planning over months,' said the girl, smiling at him. 'We did it in secret with a lot of coming and going across the border because I was determined to settle with Brix for grabbing my old man's land. We smuggled dynamite in and stored it and kept the place well staked out. This old ghost-town was ideal because we could look down on the ridge trail and the basin and spot any

Slanted B people well before they arrived. There were always look-outs, well hidden up on the roofs. That's a point you missed, Mr Clennan, though I hesitate to say you're slow on the uptake, even if I did once say you were dumb, like all men.' She gave Clennan a dusty, twinkle-eyed and mischievous smile.

Hell, thought Clennan, *that's the kind of smile a man could bask in!*

'Well, we waited our chance and moved in on Brix's mine workings by a torturous route to avoid most of the Slanted B land,' explained Daphne. 'We'd only just returned from blowing Brix's ore mine to hell when we heard a mess of shooting away down in the basin and took a hand when you reached the top of the ridge trail.'

Clennan winced as she sloshed iodine into his freshly cleaned wound. 'You're the darndest lady I ever knew – specially for one with a fancy name like Daphne,' he observed.

'Well, you never knew my old man and the way he brought me up,' she informed him. 'He gave me a good education in spite of his struggles. He encouraged me to go my own way and I guess I was a bit of a tomboy, but I chose to take up nursing and he still followed the dreams of his youth – always hoping to start a modest ranch out here in the west. He was a small-time farmer in Iowa and my mother died when I was young. Eventually, he made enough to buy his little place, nudging the Slanted B holdings. He ran it with a couple of hands until Brix got word of a silver-lode in the

152

rocky slopes there.'

She placed a lint pad on Clennan's wound with a deft, professional touch. 'I went to work in Mexico with a charity when there was an epidemic there and stayed awhile,' she said. 'You'll know that, down there, they have a president named Don Porfirio Diaz, who is anything but gentle and I guess you've heard of Santa Rosarita.'

'Sure, the place in Sonora where Diaz's *federale* troops put down an attempt at revolution. It was a massacre.'

'It was, and I helped nurse survivors who escaped to safety. If I say so myself, I earned the gratitude of some tough revolutionaries – the kind who'll surely end Diaz's rule one day soon.' She waved towards the Mexicans in the cave. 'Take a look at them – men like Nacio, an intellectual and a man of the earth, the kind you want beside you in tight corners.'

Lars Lundgren accepted a refill of coffee from a Mexican. 'I know the kind,' he interjected. 'The silent Mexican, tough as nails, patient and with a burning sense of justice and they make good coffee, too.'

'And I guess Brix's exploiting Mexican and Indian labour at his mine didn't sit well with your friends,' commented Clennan.

'No. And they know secret ways through the border. Most are of Indian stock and they know this country better than most Americans. After all, it was all their land once and they never recognized international borders,' Daphne said. 'They also have contacts with sources in the United States sympathetic to a Mexican revolution. That's where our dynamite came from.' She produced a clean bandage from her supplies. 'You should rest, Mr Clennan. You're about all in.'

'Not until I'm through with some further chores. I want to borrow a fresh horse from you and call at the bank in Brimstone to collect an important document,' said Clennan.

She shook her head and smiled again. 'You're a pretty determined man, Mr Clennan,' she observed.

'Coming from you, that's some compliment,' he answered, somewhat absently for he was finding an enchanting magic in her smile.

Yes, he reflected again, *a man could bask in that smile.*

Lew Clennan and Lars Lundgren, mounted on fresh animals borrowed from their Mexican allies, were heading out of Kimmins City in the direction of the ridge trail and Brimstone. It was now past noon, they had rested for a couple of hours and were intent on urgent business.

Still drowsy, Clennan was trying to formulate mentally the tasks he wished to tackle. Most important, he must visit the US marshal in Tucson with the lawyer Tait's confession verifying Brix's engineering of the deaths of his father and brothers and his machinations in obtaining the MC outfit; he needed legal advice concerning regaining the MC and he needed to contact Ted Orme since he knew the whereabouts of former MC hands willing to return to their old outfit. Then there was the important business of helping Lars get back on his feet with a restored horse ranch, which would also entail an attempt to catch his run-off horseflesh which must by now be scattered to the winds.

He was so deep in his thoughts that he hardly heard Lars say: 'Lew, you know, that girl back at the cave—'

Clennan cut him off, coming out of his weariness with a sudden gasping cry. His hand flew for the butt of his holstered pistol.

Two mounted figures were jogging towards them out of the sun-sparkled dust of the trail – two stark, big-hatted figures in duster coats.

'Hell!' spluttered Clennan. 'The Trilling agents! I'd forgotten about them. And they're looking for me!'

'I know it. I've already met them and they'll be good and mad at me,' growled Lars, also grabbing for his sixgun.

Reeder, the taller and skinnier of the approaching pair, suddenly spurred his horse and sent it forward at a trot. To the astonishment of Clennan and Lundgren, who had now drawn their guns, he raised both his hands and bawled: 'Don't shoot! Don't shoot!'

'You're looking for me, aren't you?' roared Clennan.

Reeder came closer and responded: 'Not any more. We learned things, thanks to the telegraph. There's no reward out for you.' He halted his animal as he reached Clennan. 'The folks of Purple Flats got sick of the cattle company running the place. They were a gang of crooks so the folks up and kicked 'em out. It'd been brewing for a long time and the townsfolk formed a committee and sent the company men and the lawmen in their pockets running. They formed a new town council and got rid of the dubious warrants put out by the previous bunch, including the one out for you.

'That son of a company boss you shot had been getting away with terrorizing folks for too long. If you go back, I reckon they'll elect you mayor. The offer of a reward was withdrawn and, since the Trilling Detective Agency don't exert itself when there's no reward, we're moving on.'

'And,' put in Slip Corkery from the midst of his prodigious moustache, 'we know you didn't rob the bank in Brimstone. The president came out and calmed everyone. Said you'd been in there on legitimate business. That lawyer who was doing all the shouting seems to have left town. He must have been drunk or plumb loco.'

'Sure, there's all hell going on in the basin,' said Reeder. 'We hear Brix is dead and we met up with some damned dejected Slanted B men with the corpses of others over their saddles, taking them off for burial. Marshal Wiseman is lying low someplace. Still, it's none of our business now – there's no reward in any of it.'

'No, we have other things to do,' drawled the lugubrious Corkery. 'Headquarters told us by telegraph there's a couple of jokers needing to be caught – with a big reward out for 'em.'

'A couple of jokers up in Utah,' Reeder said. 'Are we headed the right way for Utah?'

'Sure, more or less,' Clennan confirmed.

Reeder raised a parting hand, Corkery nodded a farewell and the pair spurred their animals.

As the Trilling men moved off, Clennan and Lundgren heard Reeder complaining: 'We wouldn't have to ask directions if you hadn't lost my good army map.'

The pair dwindled in their backtrail with Corkery replying: 'I never laid a finger on your blamed map. If it's lost, you're the one who lost it. . . .'

Clennan and Lundgren resumed their ride and Clennan urged: 'C'mon. Let's hustle. I want to get to Jeff Samson before he closes the bank for the day, among other things. What was that you were saying a few minutes ago?'

'I was commenting on that girl, Daphne,' said Lars. 'I was about to say she's a hell of a woman, all spirit and fire and knows what she wants. There's not many like her.'

'I know it.'

'And I was about to say: when it comes to picking a man that girl will go for her own kind – one who knows what he's aiming for and has the guts to get up and push for it, come hell or high water,' rumbled the old Swede.

'Are you trying to make some kind of point?' asked Clennan impatiently.

'Only that I saw the way she smiled at you more than once and the last time I saw that kind of smile it was on the face of the girl I should have married, only I was a damned fool and I took off, got myself in a mess of trouble and finally figured she was far too good for me.' Lars sighed, then added: 'That's an almighty fetching and promising smile to put before a man.'

Clennan answered: 'Do you think I don't know it? Why do you figure I'm in such an all-fired hurry to clear up our immediate business and get back to that cave?'

He grinned and looked ahead towards a sun-washed Tinkettle Basin which had taken on a new attraction, nearly as fetching and promising as Daphne's smile.